# THE RANDOM HOUSE BOOK
## OF
# BEDTIME STORIES

# The Random House Book of Bedtime Stories

ILLUSTRATED BY

## Jane Dyer

RANDOM HOUSE 🏠 NEW YORK

*To Tom with love*

Compilation copyright © 1994 by Random House, Inc.
Illustrations copyright © 1994 by Jane Dyer.
All rights reserved under International and Pan-American Copyright Conventions.
Published in the United States by Random House, Inc., New York,
and simultaneously in Canada by Random House of Canada Limited, Toronto.

All acknowledgments for permission to reprint previously published material
can be found on page 139.

*Library of Congress Cataloging-in-Publication Data*
The Random House book of bedtime stories / illustrated by Jane Dyer.
p.   cm.   SUMMARY: A collection of original and traditional stories, including
"The Selfish Giant," "The Golden Goose," and "The Tale of Peter Rabbit."
ISBN 0-679-80832-9 (trade) — ISBN 0-679-90832-3 (lib. bdg.)
1. Children's stories.   2. Tales.   [1. Short stories.   2. Folklore.]
I. Dyer, Jane, ill.   II. Random House (Firm)
PZ5.R1935   1994   [E]—dc20   94-2631

Manufactured in the United States of America   10 9 8 7 6 5 4 3 2 1

# CONTENTS

# THE
# RANDOM
# HOUSE
# BOOK OF
# BEDTIME
# STORIES

# How
# the Camel Got His Hump

## by Rudyard Kipling

N ow this is the next tale, and it tells how the Camel got his big hump.

In the beginning of years, when the world was so new-and-all, and the Animals were just beginning to work for Man, there was a Camel, and he lived in the middle of a Howling Desert because he did not want to work; and besides, he was a Howler himself. So he ate sticks and thorns and tamarisks and milkweed and prickles, most 'scruciating idle; and when anybody spoke to him he said "Humph!" Just "Humph!" and no more.

Presently the Horse came to him on Monday morning, with a saddle on his back and a bit in his mouth, and said, "Camel, O Camel, come out and trot like the rest of us."

"Humph!" said the Camel, and the Horse went away and told the Man.

Presently the Dog came to him, with a stick in his mouth, and said, "Camel, O Camel, come and fetch and carry like the rest of us."

"Humph!" said the Camel, and the Dog went away and told the Man.

Presently the Ox came to him, with the yoke on his neck,

and said, "Camel, O Camel, come and plow like the rest of us."

"Humph!" said the Camel, and the Ox went away and told the Man.

At the end of the day the Man called the Horse and the Dog and the Ox together, and said, "Three, O Three, I'm very sorry for you—with the world so new-and-all—but that Humph-thing in the Desert can't work, or he would have been here by now, so I am going to leave him alone, and you must work double time to make up for it."

That made the Three very angry (with the world so new-and-all), and they held a palaver and an indaba and a pun-chayet and a powwow on the edge of the Desert, and the Camel came chewing milkweed most 'scruciating idle and laughed at them. Then he said "Humph!" and went away again.

Presently there came along the Jinn in charge of All Deserts, rolling in a cloud of dust (Jinns always travel that way because it is Magic), and he stopped to palaver and powwow with the Three.

"Jinn of All Deserts," said the Horse, "*is* it right for anyone to be idle, with the world so new-and-all?"

"Certainly not," said the Jinn.

"Well," said the Horse, "there's a thing in the middle of your Howling Desert—and he's a Howler himself—with a long neck and long legs, and he hasn't done a stroke of work since Monday morning. He won't trot."

"Whew!" said the Jinn, whistling. "That's my Camel, for all the gold in Arabia! What does he say about it?"

"He says, 'Humph!' " said the Dog, "and he won't fetch and carry."

"Does he say anything else?"

"Only 'Humph!' And he won't plow," said the Ox.

"Very good," said the Jinn. "I'll humph him if you will kindly wait a minute."

The Jinn rolled himself up in his dust cloak and took a bearing across the desert and found the Camel most 'scruciatingly idle, looking at his own reflection in a pool of water.

"My long and bubbling friend," said the Jinn, "what's this I hear of your doing no work, with the world so new-and-all?"

"Humph!" said the Camel.

The Jinn sat down with his chin in his hand and began to think a Great Magic, while the Camel looked at his own reflection in the pool of water.

"You've given the Three extra work ever since Monday morning, all on account of your 'scruciating idleness," said the Jinn, and he went on thinking Magics with his chin in his hand.

"Humph!" said the Camel.

"I shouldn't say that again if I were you," said the Jinn. "You might say it once too often. Bubbles, I want you to work."

And the Camel said "Humph!" again. But no sooner had he said it than he saw his back that he was so proud of puffing up and puffing up into a great big lolloping humph.

"Do you see that?" said the Jinn. "That's your very own humph that you've brought upon your very own self by not working. Today is Thursday, and you've done no work since Monday, when the work began. Now you are going to work."

"How can I," said the Camel, "with this humph on my back?"

# How the Camel Got His Hump

"That's made a-purpose," said the Jinn, "all because you missed those three days. You will be able to work now for three days without eating because you can live on your humph. And don't you ever say I never did anything for you. Come out of the Desert and go to the Three, and behave. Humph yourself!"

And the Camel humphed himself, humph and all, and went away to join the Three. And from that day to this the Camel always wears a humph (we call it "hump" now, not to hurt his feelings), but he has never yet caught up with the three days that he missed at the beginning of the world, and he has never yet learned how to behave.

# THE LION AND THE MOUSE

## by Aesop

A lion was asleep in his den one day when a mischievous mouse for no reason at all ran across the outstretched paw and up the royal nose of the king of beasts, awakening him from his nap. The mighty beast clapped his paw upon the now thoroughly frightened little creature and would have made an end of him.

"Please," squealed the mouse, "don't kill me. Forgive me this time, O King, and I shall never forget it. A day may come, who knows, when I may do you a good turn to repay your kindness."

The lion, smiling at his little prisoner's fright and amused by the thought that so small a creature could ever be of assistance to the king of beasts, let him go.

Not long afterward the lion, while ranging the forest for his prey, was caught in a net that a hunter had set to catch him. He let out a roar that echoed through the forest. Even the mouse heard it and, recognizing the voice of his former preserver and friend, ran to the spot where the lion lay tangled in the net of ropes.

"Well, Your Majesty," said the mouse, "I know you did not believe me when I said I would return a kindness, but here is my chance."

And without further ado he set to work to nibble with his sharp little teeth at the ropes that bound the lion. Soon the lion was able to crawl out of the hunter's snare and be free.

MORAL: *No act of kindness, no matter how small, is ever wasted.*

# THE TALE
# OF PETER RABBIT

## by Beatrix Potter

Once upon a time there were four little rabbits, and their names were Flopsy, Mopsy, Cotton-tail, and Peter.

They lived with their mother in a sandbank underneath the root of a very big fir tree.

"Now, my dears," said old Mrs. Rabbit one morning, "you may go into the fields or down the lane. But don't go into Mr. McGregor's garden. Your father had an accident there; he was put in a pie by Mrs. McGregor. Now run along, and don't get into mischief. I am going out."

Then old Mrs. Rabbit took a basket and her umbrella and went through the wood to the baker's. She bought a loaf of brown bread and five currant buns.

Flopsy, Mopsy, and Cotton-tail, who were good little bunnies, went down the lane to gather blackberries, but Peter, who was naughty, ran straight away to Mr. McGregor's garden and squeezed under the gate!

First he ate some lettuce and some beans. Then he ate some radishes. Then, feeling rather sick, he went to look for some parsley.

But around the end of a cucumber frame, whom should he meet but Mr. McGregor!

Mr. McGregor was on his hands and knees planting out young cabbages, but he jumped up and ran after Peter, waving a rake and calling out, "Stop, thief!"

Peter was dreadfully frightened. He rushed all over the garden, for he had forgotten the way back to the gate.

He lost one of his shoes among the cabbages and the other shoe among the potatoes.

After losing them he ran on four legs and went faster, so that I think he might have got away altogether if he had not unfortunately run into a gooseberry net and got caught by the large buttons on his jacket. It was a blue jacket with brass buttons, quite new.

Peter gave himself up for lost and shed big tears, but his sobs were overheard by some friendly sparrows, who flew to him in great excitement, and implored him to exert himself.

Mr. McGregor came up with a sieve, which he intended to pop upon the top of Peter, but Peter wriggled out just in time, leaving his jacket behind him, and rushed into the toolshed and jumped into a can. It would have been a beautiful thing to hide in if it had not had so much water in it.

Mr. McGregor was quite sure that Peter was somewhere

in the toolshed, perhaps hidden underneath a flowerpot. He began to turn them over carefully, looking under each.

Presently Peter sneezed—"Kertyschoo!" Mr. McGregor was after him in no time, and tried to put his foot upon Peter, who jumped out of a window, upsetting three plants. The window was too small for Mr. McGregor, and he was tired of running after Peter. He went back to his work.

Peter sat down to rest. He was out of breath and trembling with fright, and he had not the least idea which way to go.

Also, he was very damp from sitting in that can.

After a time he began to wander about, going lippity-lippity—not very fast, and looking all around.

He found a door in a wall, but it was locked, and there was no room for a fat little rabbit to squeeze underneath.

An old mouse was running in and out over the stone doorstep, carrying peas and beans to her family in the wood. Peter asked her the way to the gate, but she had such a large pea in her mouth that she could not answer. She only shook her head at him. Peter began to cry.

Then he tried to find his way straight across the garden, but he became more and more puzzled. Presently he came to a pond where Mr. McGregor filled his water cans.

A white cat was staring at some goldfish. She sat very, very still, but now and then the tip of her tail twitched as if it were alive.

Peter thought it best to go away without speaking to her; he had heard about cats from his cousin, Benjamin Bunny.

He went back towards the toolshed, but suddenly, quite close to him, he heard a noise of a hoe—scr-r-ritch, scratch, scratch, scritch. Peter scuttled underneath the bushes.

But presently, as nothing happened, he came out and climbed upon a wheelbarrow and peeped over. The first thing he saw was Mr. McGregor hoeing onions. His back was towards Peter, and beyond him was the gate!

Peter got down very quietly off the wheelbarrow and started running as fast as he could go along a straight walk behind some black-currant bushes.

Mr. McGregor caught sight of him at the corner, but Peter did not care. He slipped underneath the gate and was safe at last in the wood outside the garden.

Mr. McGregor hung up the little jacket and the shoes for a scarecrow to frighten the blackbirds.

Peter never stopped running or looked behind him till he got home to the big fir tree.

He was so tired that he flopped down upon the nice soft sand on the floor of the rabbit hole and shut his eyes.

His mother was busy cooking; she wondered what he had done with his clothes. It was the second little jacket and pair of shoes that Peter had lost in a fortnight!

I am sorry to say that Peter was not very well during the evening.

His mother put him to bed and made some chamomile tea, and she gave a dose of it to Peter! "One tablespoonful to be taken at bedtime."

But Flopsy, Mopsy, and Cotton-tail had bread and milk and blackberries for supper.

# THE SELFISH GIANT

## by Oscar Wilde

Every afternoon, as they were coming from school, the children used to go and play in the giant's garden.

It was a large lovely garden with soft green grass. Here and there over the grass stood beautiful flowers like stars, and there were twelve peach-trees that in the spring-time broke out into delicate blossoms of pink and pearl and in the autumn bore rich fruit. The birds sat on the trees and sang so sweetly that the children used to stop their games in order to listen to them. "How happy we are here!" they cried to each other.

One day the giant came back. He had been to visit his friend the ogre, and had stayed with him for seven years. When he arrived he saw the children playing in the garden.

"What are you doing here?" he cried in a very gruff voice, and the children ran away.

"My own garden is my own garden," said the giant. "I will allow nobody to play in it but myself." So he built a high wall all around it and put up a notice board.

**Trespassers Will Be Prosecuted**

13

He was a very selfish giant.

The poor children had now nowhere to play. They tried to play on the road, but the road was very dusty and full of hard stones, and they did not like it. They used to wander around the high walls when their lessons were over, and talk about the beautiful garden inside. "How happy we were there!" they said to each other.

Then the Spring came, and all over the country there were little blossoms and little birds. Only in the garden of the selfish giant it was still winter. The birds did not care to sing in it as there were no children, and the trees forgot to blossom. Once a beautiful flower put its head out from the grass, but when it saw the notice board it was so sorry for the children that it slipped back into the ground again, and went off to sleep. The only people who were pleased were the Snow and the Frost.

"Spring has forgotten this garden," they cried, "so we will live here all the year round."

The Snow covered up the grass with her great white cloak, and the Frost painted all the trees silver. Then they invited the North Wind to stay with them, and he came. He was wrapped in furs, and he roared all day about the garden, and blew the chimney-pots down.

"This is a delightful spot," he said, "we must ask the Hail on a visit."

So the Hail came. Every day for three hours he rattled on the roof of the castle till he broke most of the slates, and then he ran around and around the garden as fast as he could go. He was dressed in grey, and his breath was like ice.

"I cannot understand why the Spring is so late in coming," said the selfish giant, as he sat at the window and looked out at his cold, white garden. "I hope there will be a change in the weather."

But the Spring never came, nor the Summer. The Autumn gave golden fruit to every garden, but to the giant's garden she gave none.

"He is too selfish," she said. So it was always winter there, and the North Wind and the Hail, and the Frost, and the Snow danced about through the trees.

One morning the giant was lying awake in bed when he heard some lovely music. It sounded so sweet to his ears that he thought it must be the king's musicians passing by. It was really only a little linnet singing outside his window, but it was so long since he had heard a bird sing in his garden that it seemed to him to be the most beautiful music in the world.

Then the Hail stopped dancing over his head, and the North Wind ceased roaring, and a delicious perfume came to him through the open window. "I believe the Spring has come at last," said the giant, and he jumped out of bed and looked out.

What did he see?

He saw a most wonderful sight. Through a little hole in the wall the children had crept in, and they were sitting in the branches of the trees. In every tree that he could see there was a little child. And the trees were so glad to have the children back again that they had covered themselves with blossoms and were waving their arms gently above the children's heads. The birds were flying about and twittering with delight, and the flowers were looking up through the green grass and laughing. It was a lovely scene, only in one corner it was still Winter. It was the farthest corner of the garden, and in it was standing a little boy. He was so small that he could not reach up to the branches of the tree, and he was wandering all around it, crying bitterly. The poor tree was still covered with frost and snow, and the North Wind was blowing and roaring above it.

"Climb up, little boy!" said the tree, and bent its branches down as low as it could. But the boy was too tiny.

And the giant's heart melted as he looked out. "How selfish I have been!" he said. "Now I know why the Spring would not come here. I will put that poor little boy on the top of the tree, and then I will knock down the wall, and my garden shall be the children's playground for ever and ever." He was really very sorry for what he had done.

So he crept downstairs and opened the front door quite softly, and went out into the garden. But when the children saw him they were so frightened that they all ran away, and the garden became Winter again. Only the little boy did not run, for his eyes were so full of tears that he did not see the giant coming. And the giant stole up behind him and took him gently in his hand, and put him up into the tree. And the tree broke at once into blossom, and the birds came and sang on it, and the little boy stretched out his two arms and flung them round the giant's neck, and kissed him. And the other children, when they saw that the giant was not wicked any longer, came running back, and with them came the Spring.

"It is your garden now, little children," said the giant, and he took a great axe and knocked down the wall. And when the people were going to market at twelve o'clock that day, they found the giant playing with the children in the most beautiful garden they had ever seen.

# GRUMLEY THE GROUCH

## by Marjorie Weinman Sharmat

J. Grumley Badger was the biggest grouch in the neighborhood.

Every day he found at least ten things he didn't like.

"How are you, Grumley?" his neighbor Hank Muskrat would ask politely.

"Simply terrible," Grumley would reply.

"How are things going, Grumley?" asked another neighbor, Nero Pig.

"Rotten," said Grumley. "The sun is too shiny. The rain is too wet. The grass isn't green enough. The sky is too far up."

Grumley gnashed his teeth. "And there's more," he said. "Much more."

One rainy day Grumley's house got flooded.

"I knew the rain was too wet," he muttered as he sloshed through his house.

"Slosh! Slop! And a soggy bed! Things never get better. They only get wetter."

Grumley went to Hank's house.

"I'll have to stay with you until my house dries out," he said. And he moved in.

"I always liked your place," said Grumley.

"You did?" asked Hank.

"Of course it could be better," said Grumley.

"Oh?" said Hank. "How?"

"Well, your floor squeaks," said Grumley.

"I never noticed," said Hank.

"And your mattress sags," said Grumley.

"I never noticed that either," said Hank.

"Yes, it just sags and sags," said Grumley. "Do you mind if I sleep on your floor? I prefer a squeak to a sag."

Grumley lay down on the floor. He looked up at the ceiling. "I suppose you know about your ceiling," he said.

"What about it?" asked Hank.

"It has water spots," said Grumley. "And they're very ugly."

"Take a nap, Grumley," said Hank.

"Do you expect me to nap under ugly water spots?" said Grumley. "Don't you remember what happened to my house?"

"How can I forget?" said Hank. "Your house flooded, and you came to stay with me."

"Aren't you happy to have me, Hank?" asked Grumley.

"Um," said Hank.

"Um," cried Grumley. " 'Um' means you're not happy to have me."

Grumley got up. "I'm leaving!" he said, and he walked out and slammed the door.

He went to Nero Pig's house.

"Say, Nero, did you hear about my wet house?" asked Grumley.

"Yes, and it made me so sad I couldn't eat for two hours," said Nero. "Would you like to stay with me until your house is dry?"

"I accept," said Grumley.

Grumley went inside and walked around. "I have never been inside your house," he said. "Your floors don't squeak, your ceiling looks spotless, and your mattress is firm."

"Glad you like everything," said Nero.

"I didn't say *that*," said Grumley. "Your clock ticks ferociously, there is a horrid draft from your kitchen window, and the unmistakable smell of rotting artichokes is in the air."

Nero opened a book and started to read.

"Why don't you say something?" said Grumley.

Nero kept reading.

"If you don't talk to me, I'll leave," said Grumley.

Nero read on.

"I'm leaving!" said Grumley, and he walked out and slammed the door.

He stood outside the door. He didn't know where to go next.

He started to walk. "Maybe I'll just walk around until my house dries," he thought.

Grumley walked for many miles. He was feeling very tired when he saw a house by the side of the road. He went up the front walk. There was a sign on the door. GO AWAY.

Grumley gnashed his teeth. "I do not like that sign," he said. "I do not like the way it looks. I do not like what it says. I do not like anything about it. But I am so tired that I will knock on the door anyway."

Grumley knocked.

Brunhilda Badger answered the door. She pointed to the sign. "I don't like strangers," she said.

22

"I am tired," said Grumley.

"I don't like tired strangers either," said Brunhilda.

"Well, then, I'm cold and hungry," said Grumley.

"I don't like tired or cold or hungry strangers," said Brunhilda. "And I also don't like them when they're rested, warm and fed."

"May I come in anyway?" asked Grumley.

"If you must," said Brunhilda.

Grumley walked inside and stood in front of the fireplace. "Your fire feels nice and toasty," he said.

"It's too hot," said Brunhilda.

Grumley saw some soup in a pot. "That might warm me up, too," he said.

"It's greasy and gucky," said Brunhilda.

Grumley saw a pillow on the floor. "That pillow would be fine for a weary head," he said.

"It's lumpy," said Brunhilda.

Grumley looked at Brunhilda. "Don't you like anything?" he asked.

"Well, there is so much not to like," said Brunhilda.

"I agree," said Grumley. "But there must be something you like."

"I'll think about it," said Brunhilda.

"Well . . . " said Grumley.

"It's very difficult, you know," said Brunhilda. "But I *am* thinking about it." Then she said, "I remember. Once I liked chocolate sundaes with walnuts and cherries."

"Me too," said Grumley. "With marshmallow bits on top."

"I think I'll make one," said Brunhilda.

"Two, please," said Grumley.

Grumley and Brunhilda sat in front of the fire, eating their sundaes.

Grumley said, "Something very strange is happening."

"I know it," said Brunhilda.

"I like *you*," said Grumley. "That's what's strange."

"I like you, too," said Brunhilda.

"Do you suppose there are even more things to like be-sides each other and sundaes?" asked Grumley.

"Could be," said Brunhilda. Then she said, "How about soft shirts? I like soft shirts under scratchy ones."

"I like picture frames when I have a picture," said Grumley.

"I like holes," said Brunhilda. "They're airy and cool, and you can see through them."

"I like breathing," said Grumley.

"That's a good one," said Brunhilda. "How about rain? Maybe we could like rain."

"Rain? Rain's too wet," said Grumley.

"But rain comes before a rainbow," said Brunhilda.

"I suppose," said Grumley. "There was a rainbow when I went to stay with Hank Muskrat. He let me stay in his house and on his mattress and on his floor."

"I could like Hank," said Brunhilda.

"Yes, Hank is somebody to like," said Grumley. "And Nero Pig also said I could stay with him. He couldn't eat for two hours when he heard about my soaked house."

"I could like Nero, too," said Brunhilda.

"Yes, so could I," said Grumley.

"Let's tell Hank and Nero," said Brunhilda.

"It's a long walk to their houses," said Grumley.

"I think I like long walks," said Brunhilda.

"I think I do, too," said Grumley.

Grumley and Brunhilda started to walk.

"I'm definitely liking this," said Grumley as they walked along.

"Yes," said Brunhilda. "The pebbles and the trees are all first-rate."

"The dirt under our feet isn't bad at all," said Grumley.

"And let's not forget the clouds up there," said Brunhilda. "They remind me a bit of soft shirts, and I know I like soft shirts."

"I like the company the best of all," said Grumley.

"Yes. The very best of all," said Brunhilda.

Suddenly Grumley saw Hank and Nero sitting in front of Nero's house. Grumley and Brunhilda ran up to them.

"We were just talking about you, Grumley," said Nero. "We think you're the biggest grouch in the neighborhood."

"No doubt about it," said Hank.

"No, he's not," said Brunhilda. "He likes dirt and sundaes and me, Brunhilda, and picture frames and all kinds of things."

"How about sagging mattresses?" asked Hank.

"And the unmistakable smell of rotting artichokes?" asked Nero.

"Well, maybe," said Grumley. "But not as much as I like all of you."

Hank and Nero put their heads together and whispered.

"That doesn't sound like a grouch talking," said Nero.

"That's positively nongrouch talk," said Hank.

"Let's all go to my house for good conversation and chocolate sundaes," said Grumley. "My house must be dry by now."

Grumley, Brunhilda, Hank, and Nero went to Grumley's house and stepped inside.

The floor was still flooded. Water dripped from the ceiling.

Grumley sloshed around.

"Well, well, well, it's still not quite dry," he said cheerfully.

"Dry isn't everything," said Brunhilda as she wrung out her dress. "Let's all sit on this soggy sofa and enjoy our sundaes."

Two months later, when the house dried out, Brunhilda and Grumley got married.

Grumley became less and less grouchy as the years went by, but still . . .

He never became terribly fond of rain.

# THE BAKER'S CAT

## by Joan Aiken

nce there was an old lady, Mrs. Jones, who lived with her cat, Mog. Mrs. Jones kept a baker's shop in a little tiny town at the bottom of a valley between two mountains.

Every morning you could see Mrs. Jones's light twinkling long before all the other houses in the town, because she got up very early to bake loaves and buns and jam tarts and Welsh cakes.

First thing in the morning Mrs. Jones lit a big fire. Then she made dough out of water and sugar and yeast. Then she put the dough into pans and set it in front of the fire to rise.

Mog got up early too. *He* got up to catch mice. When he had chased all the mice out of the bakery, he wanted to sit in front of the warm fire. But Mrs. Jones wouldn't let him, because of the loaves and buns there, rising in their pans.

She said, "Don't sit on the buns, Mog."

The buns were rising nicely. They were getting fine and big. That is what yeast does. It makes the bread and buns and cakes swell up and get bigger and bigger.

As Mog was not allowed to sit by the fire, he went to play in the sink.

Most cats hate water, but Mog didn't. He loved it. He liked to sit by the tap, hitting the drops with his paw as they fell and getting water all over his whiskers!

What did Mog look like? His back and his sides and his legs down as far as where his socks would have come to and his face and ears and his tail were all marmalade colored. His stomach and his waistcoat and his paws were white. And he had a white tassel at the tip of his tail, white fringes to his ears, and white whiskers. The water made his marmalade fur go almost fox color and his paws and waistcoat shining-white clean.

But Mrs. Jones said, "Mog, you are getting too excited. You are shaking water all over my pans of buns just when they are getting nice and big. Run along and play outside."

Mog was affronted. He put his ears and tail down (when cats are pleased they put their ears and tails *up*), and he went out. It was raining hard.

29

A rushing, rocky river ran through the middle of the town. Mog went and sat *in* the water and looked for fish. But there were no fish in that part of the river. Mog got wetter and wetter. But he didn't care. Presently he began to sneeze.

Then Mrs. Jones opened her door and called, "Mog! I have put the buns in the oven. You can come in now and sit by the fire."

Mog was so wet that he was shiny all over, as if he had been polished. As he sat by the fire he sneezed nine times.

Mrs. Jones said, "Oh, dear, Mog, are you catching a cold?"

She dried him with a towel and gave him some warm milk with yeast in it. Yeast is good for people when they are ill.

Then she left him sitting in front of the fire and began making jam tarts. When she had put the tarts in the oven she went out shopping, taking her umbrella.

But what do you think was happening to Mog?

The yeast was making him rise.

As he sat dozing in front of the lovely warm fire he was growing bigger and bigger.

First he grew as big as a sheep.

Then he grew as big as a donkey.

Then he grew as big as a cart horse.

Then he grew as big as a hippopotamus.

By now he was too big for Mrs. Jones's little kitchen, but he was *far* too big to get through the door. He just burst the walls.

When Mrs. Jones came home with her shopping bag and her umbrella she cried out, "Mercy me, what is happening to my house?"

The whole house was bulging. It was swaying. Huge whiskers were poking out of the kitchen window. A marmalade-colored tail came out the door. A white paw came out one bedroom window and an ear with a white fringe out the other.

"Meow?" said Mog. He was waking up from his nap and trying to stretch.

Then the whole house fell down.

"Oh, Mog!" cried Mrs. Jones. "*Look* what you've done."

31

The people in the town were very astonished when they saw what had happened. They gave Mrs. Jones the town hall to live in, because they were so fond of her (and her buns). But they were not so sure about Mog.

The mayor said, "Suppose he goes on growing and breaks our town hall? Suppose he turns fierce? It would not be safe to have him in the town. He is too big."

Mrs. Jones said, "Mog is a gentle cat. He would not hurt anybody."

"We will wait and see about that," said the mayor. "Suppose he sat down on someone? Suppose he was hungry? What will he eat? He had better live outside the town, up on the mountain."

So everybody shouted, "Shoo! Scram! Pssst! Shoo!" And poor Mog was driven outside the town gates. It was still raining hard. Water was rushing down the mountains. Not that Mog cared.

But poor Mrs. Jones was very sad. She began making a new batch of loaves and buns in the town hall, crying into them so much that the dough was too wet and very salty.

Mog walked up the valley between the two mountains. By now he was bigger than an elephant—almost as big as a whale! When the sheep on the mountain saw him coming, they were scared to death and galloped away. But he took no notice of them. He was looking for fish in the river. He caught lots of fish! He was having a fine time.

By now it had been raining for so long that Mog heard a loud, watery roar at the top of the valley. He saw a huge wall of water coming toward him. The river was beginning to flood as more and more rainwater poured down into it off the mountains.

Mog thought, "If I don't stop that water, all these fine fish will be washed away."

So he sat down, plump in the middle of the valley, and he spread himself out like a big fat cottage loaf.

The water could not get by.

The people in the town had heard the roar of the floodwater. They were very frightened. The mayor shouted, "Run up the mountains before the water gets to the town, or we shall all be drowned!"

So they all rushed up the mountains, some on one side of the town, some on the other.

What did they see then?

Why, Mog, sitting in the middle of the valley. Beyond him was a great lake.

"Mrs. Jones," said the mayor, "can you make your cat stay there till we have built a dam across the valley to keep all that water back?"

"I will try," said Mrs. Jones. "He mostly sits still if he is tickled under his chin."

So for three days everybody in the town took turns tickling Mog under his chin with hay rakes. He purred and purred and purred. His purring made big waves roll right across the the lake of floodwater.

All this time the best builders were making a great dam across the valley.

People brought Mog all sorts of nice things to eat, too—bowls of cream and condensed milk, liver and bacon, sardines,

even chocolate! But he was not very hungry. He had eaten so much fish.

On the third day they finished the dam. The town was safe.

The mayor said, "I see now that Mog is a gentle cat. He can live in the town hall with you, Mrs. Jones. Here is a badge for him to wear."

The badge was on a silver chain to go around his neck. It said MOG SAVED OUR TOWN.

So Mrs. Jones and Mog lived happily ever after in the town hall. If you go to the little town of Carnmog you will see the policeman holding up the traffic while Mog walks through the streets on his way to catch fish in the lake for breakfast. His tail waves above the houses and his whiskers rattle against the upstairs windows. But people know he will not hurt them, because he is a gentle cat.

He loves to play in the lake, and sometimes he gets so wet that he sneezes. But Mrs. Jones is not going to give him any more yeast.

He is quite big enough already!

# THE LAD WHO WENT TO THE NORTH WIND

## by Anne Rockwell

nce upon a time there was a widow who had one son, and he went out to the storehouse to fetch some oatmeal for cooking. But as he was coming back to the house there came the North Wind, puffing and blowing. The North Wind caught up the oatmeal and blew it away. Then the lad went back to the storehouse for more, but no sooner had he come outside than the North Wind came and blew away the oatmeal with just one puff. Worse yet, the Wind did it a third time.

At this the lad got very angry, and as he thought it mean that the North Wind should behave so, he decided he'd go and find the North Wind and ask him to give back the oatmeal.

So off he went, but the way was long, and he walked and he walked, but at last he came to the North Wind's house.

"Good day," said the lad. "Thank you for coming to see us yesterday."

"Good day!" answered the North Wind in a loud, gruff voice. "Thanks for coming to see me. What do you want?"

"Oh," said the lad, "I only wished to ask you to be so kind as to let me have back that oatmeal you took from me, for my mother and I haven't much to live on. If you're to go on snapping up every morsel we have, we'll starve."

"I haven't got your oatmeal," said the North Wind, "but if you are in such need, I'll give you a cloth which will give you all the food you want if you will only say, 'Cloth, cloth, spread yourself and serve up a good dinner!'"

With this the lad was happy. But as the way was so long he couldn't get home in one day, he stopped overnight at an inn. He went to sit down to supper, and he laid the cloth on a table and said, "Cloth, cloth, spread yourself and serve up a good dinner!"

And the cloth did.

Everyone at the inn thought this was a wonderful thing, but most of all the landlady. So when everyone was fast asleep, she took the lad's cloth and put another in its place. It looked just like the one the lad had got from the North Wind, but it couldn't serve up even a bit of stale bread.

When the lad woke, he took his cloth and went home to his mother.

"Now," said he, "I've been to the North Wind's house, and a good fellow he is. He gave me this cloth, and when I say to it, 'Cloth, cloth, spread yourself and serve up a good dinner!' I can get all the food I want."

"Seeing is believing," said his mother. "I shan't believe it until I see it."

So the lad made haste and laid the cloth on the table. Then he said, "Cloth, cloth, spread yourself and serve up a good dinner!"

But the cloth served up nothing, not even a bit of stale bread.

"Well," said the lad, "there is nothing to do but to go to the North Wind again." And away he went.

So he walked and he walked, and late in the afternoon he came to where the North Wind lived.

"Good evening," said the lad.

"Good evening," said the North Wind in a loud, gruff voice.

"I want my rights for that oatmeal of ours you took," said the lad. "As for the cloth I got from you, it isn't worth a penny."

"I've got no oatmeal," said the North Wind. "But I'll give you a goat which gives forth golden coins whenever you say to it, 'Goat, goat, make money!'"

So the lad thought this a fine thing, but it was too far to get home that day, so he turned in for the night at the same inn where he had slept before.

When he was settled, he tried out the goat the North Wind had given him and found it all right, but when the landlord saw the goat give forth golden coins, he changed it for an ordinary goat while the lad slept.

Next morning off went the lad. When he got home, he said to his mother, "What a good fellow the North Wind is! Now he has given me a goat that gives forth golden coins whenever I say, 'Goat, goat, make money!'"

"All very true, I daresay," said his mother. "But I shan't believe it until I see the gold coins made."

"Goat, goat, make money!" said the lad, but the goat didn't.

So the lad went back to the North Wind and got very angry, for he said the goat was worth nothing and he must have his oatmeal back.

"Well," said the North Wind, "I've nothing else to give you except that old stick in the corner, but it's a stick that if you say, 'Stick, stick, lay on!' lays on until you say, 'Stick, stick, now stop!'"

So, as the way was long, the lad turned in for the night at the same inn. By now he had pretty well guessed what had become of the cloth and the goat, so he lay down on the bed and began to snore, pretending to be asleep.

Now the landlord, who was sure the stick must be worth something, found one just like it. When he heard the lad snore, he was going to exchange the two, but just as he was about to take the stick the lad yelled out, "Stick, stick, lay on!"

So the stick began to beat the landlord, and the landlord jumped over tables, chairs, and benches and yelled and roared, "Oh, my! Oh, my! Bid the stick be still, and you shall have both your cloth and your goat!"

So the lad said, "Stick, stick, now stop!"

Then he took the cloth, put it in his pocket, and went home with his stick in his hand, leading the goat by a rope, and so he got his rights for the oatmeal he had lost, and if he didn't live happily ever after, that's not the fault of either you or me.

# Under the Moon

## by Joanne Ryder

ne bright, clear evening Mama Mouse led her youngest mouse from place to place to teach her special things.

She showed her where to find the fattest seeds and the sweetest berries to eat.

She showed her tiny places under logs and snug spots inside bushes where she could hide when the owl flew by.

And then Mama said to her little mouse, "Let's go home now. Do you know where home is, little one?"

"Oh, yes, I know," said the little mouse. "We live under the moon."

"Under the moon!" said her mama. "Why, yes, I guess we do. But a little mouse needs to know more than that.

"Tell me, little one, can you remember what it smells like in our home under the moon?"

"I remember tingly smells," said the little mouse, "like the smell of warm blackberries in the sun and the smell of cool grass after the rain."

"Does it smell like that here?" asked Mama.

"No," said the little mouse, wiggling her nose and sniffing the leaves and moss and the brown roots that curled in and out of the ground. "It smells old and damp."

"You're right," said Mama. "This is the woods, and we don't live here.

"Can you tell me, little one," said Mama, "what it sounds like at home?"

"I remember singing," said the little mouse. "Tiny crickets chirp and chirp all night long at home."

"What else?" asked her mama.

"The wind," said the very small mouse. "I remember the wind whispering through the grass."

"Do you hear those things here?" asked her mama.

"No," said the little mouse. "I hear water bubbling over rocks and someone fast splashing in the water."

"Very good," said her mama. "This is the stream, and we don't live here.

"Can you tell me what it feels like when you're home?" asked Mama Mouse.

"It is warm at home," said the little mouse, "warm and soft. There are small furry mice all around me. They tickle me with their whiskers, and they touch me with their soft paws.

"I know I live in a soft place under the moon."

"Is it soft here?" asked her mama.

"No," said the little mouse. "It is hard and rough here. Sharp pebbles slip under my feet, and it is empty all around."

Just then the little mouse heard a roar, and she and her mama leaped from the rocky place into a bush as something loud rushed past.

"This is a road," said her mama. "No animals live here. Remember, little one! This is not a safe place for you.

"It is getting late," said Mama, and she led the tiny mouse

up and up, over a hilly place. They ran from bush to bush, stopping to rest under the biggest one.

The little mouse peeked between the branches and saw the stars twinkling far away. When the wind came and tickled the leaves, she saw the bright moon shining high above her.

"Look, Mama," she whispered. "It's our moon."

"Yes, it is," said her mama. "Come, little one." And they ran down the hill to the place where the grasses grew tall.

The little mouse ran and ran through the tall grass. It felt good to run here.

"What do you smell, little one?" asked her mama.

"Blackberries and grass," said the little mouse.

"What do you hear?" asked Mama.

"Crickets," said the little mouse. "I hear crickets chirping in the grass all around."

"This is the meadow, little mouse," said Mama. "Do you remember the meadow now?"

"Oh, yes," said her youngest mouse. "I remember. The meadow is the grassy place

where it smells sweet like blackberries

and where the crickets sing

and where there is a warm nest

with soft, furry mice squeaking for us to come.

Oh, Mama, I hear them calling."

"So, little one," asked her mama, "do you know where you live now?"

"I live here!" said the little mouse. "I live here in the meadow . . . under the moon."

# Young Kate

## by Eleanor Farjeon

A long time ago old Miss Daw lived in a narrow house on the edge of the town, and Young Kate was her little servant. One day Kate was sent up to clean the attic windows, and as she cleaned them she could see all the meadows that lay outside the town. So when her work was done she said to Miss Daw, "Mistress, may I go out to the meadows?"

"Oh, no!" said Miss Daw. "You mustn't go in the meadows."

"Why not, Mistress?"

"Because you might meet the Green Woman. Shut the gate, and get your mending."

The next week Kate cleaned the windows again, and as she cleaned them she saw the river that ran in the valley. So when her work was done she said to Miss Daw, "Mistress, may I go down to the river?"

"Oh, no!" said Miss Daw.

"You must never go down to the river!"

"Why ever not, Mistress?"

"Because you might meet the River King. Bar the door, and polish the brasses."

The next week when Kate cleaned the attic windows, she saw the woods that grew up the hillside, and after her work was done she went to Miss Daw and said, "Mistress, may I go up to the woods?"

"Oh, no!" said Miss Daw. "Don't ever go up to the woods!"

"Oh, Mistress, why not?"

"Because you might meet the Dancing Boy. Draw the blinds, and peel the potatoes."

Miss Daw sent Kate no more to the attic, and for six years Kate stayed in the house and mended the stockings, and polished the brass, and peeled the potatoes. Then Miss Daw died, and Kate had to find another place.

Her new place was in the town on the other side of the hills, and as Kate had no money to ride, she was obliged to walk. But she did not walk by the road. As soon as she could she went into the fields, and the first thing she saw there was the Green Woman planting flowers.

"Good morning, Young Kate," said she, "and where are you going?"

"Over the hill to the town," said Kate.

"You should have taken the road, if you meant to go quick," said the Green Woman, "for I let nobody pass through my meadows who does not stop to plant a flower."

"I'll do that willingly," said Kate, and she took the Green Woman's trowel and planted a daisy.

"Thank you," said the Green Woman. "Now pluck what you please."

Kate plucked a handful of flowers, and the Green Woman said, "For every flower you plant, you shall always pluck fifty."

Then Kate went on to the valley where the river ran, and the first thing she saw there was the River King in the reeds.

"Good day, Young Kate," said he, "and where are you going?"

"Over the hill to the town," said Kate.

"You should have kept to the road if you're in anything of a hurry," said the River King, "for I let nobody pass by my river who does not stop to sing a song."

"I will, gladly," said Kate, and she sat down in the reeds and sang.

"Thank you," said the River King. "Now listen to me."

And he sang song after song while the evening drew on, and when he had done, he kissed her and said, "For every song you sing, you shall always hear fifty."

Then Kate went up the hill to the woods on the top, and the first thing she saw there was the Dancing Boy.

"Good evening, Young Kate," said he. "Where are you going?"

"Over the hill to the town," said Kate.

"You should have kept to the road if you want to be there before morning," said the Dancing Boy, "for I let nobody through my woods who does not stop to dance."

"I will dance with joy," said Kate, and she danced her best for him.

"Thank you," said the Dancing Boy. "Now look at me."

And he danced for her till the moon came up, and danced all night till the moon went down. When morning came he

kissed her and said, "For every dance you dance, you shall always see fifty."

Young Kate then went on to the town, where in another little narrow house she became servant to old Miss Drew, who never let her go to the meadows, the woods, or the river and locked up the house at seven o'clock.

But in the course of time Young Kate married and had children and a little servant of her own. And when the day's work was done, she opened the door and said, "Run along now, children, into the meadows or down to the river or up to the hill, for I shouldn't wonder but you'll have the luck to meet the Green Woman there, or the River King, or the Dancing Boy."

And the children and the servant girl would go out, and presently Kate would see them come home again, singing and dancing with their hands full of flowers.

# Follow the Wind

## by Alvin Tresselt

T he wind blew for days and days, and nothing could stop the wind, and nothing could follow it to the end. Sometimes it was gentle and sometimes it was strong, but always it kept blowing. As it swept over the land it sang a gay little song to itself:

> "Oh, I am the wind and I do as I please,
> I blow away dust and I blow away trees.
> I huff and I bluster and sometimes I wheeze,
> Depends how I feel if I'm a gale or a breeze."

"I will follow the wind," said the kite. "I will go to the end of the wind."

His bright tail snapped, and the kite sailed up into the sky, higher and higher, over the trees and the rooftops, almost up to the clouds.

But the kite came to the end of his string before he came to the end of the wind.

"Ho, ho," laughed the wind, and blew on.

"We will float with the wind," said the white dandelion feathers when a little boy blew them to tell the time.

"We will go wherever the wind goes." They danced on the air as the wind chased them to and fro, round and around the little boy's head. But one by one they settled down in the grass.

"Whoosh," went the wind, and blew off the little boy's hat.

"I will go with the wind," said the creaking old windmill. "I will go as fast as the wind."

Slowly the windmill started turning, then faster and faster as the wind grew stronger. But no matter how fast it went, the mill was always in the same place.

And the wind laughed:

*"Oh, I am the wind and I do as I will,*
*I play with the kite or I work with the mill.*
*My voice can be low or my voice can be shrill.*
*It depends how I feel if I'm blowing or still."*

"I will fly with the wind," said the little bird, stretching his wings. "I will fly to the end of the wind."

The little bird beat his wings faster and faster, over the wide fields and meadows, farther than he had ever flown before, but the sky was so big and the wind was so strong that the little bird grew tired and rested in a shady maple tree.

The wind shook the tree's leafy branches and went on.

"I will travel with the wind," said the cloud. "I have no string to hold me and I have no wings to grow tired. I will travel across the whole great sky."

The wind blew harder and the fat white cloud scurried along with it for miles and miles over the countryside. But soon the cloud grew bigger and bigger and got so heavy it fell to the earth in a million raindrops.

Then the wind cried:

*"Oh, I am the wind and I blow the rain,*
*And when I blow hard I'm a hurricane!"*

And lightning flashed and trees tossed until the storm was over.

"I will sail with the wind," said the sailboat. "I will go until there isn't any more wind."

His white sail flapped, and the boat skimmed over the sparkling waves, past islands and fishing boats and lighthouses, but it came to a harbor before it came to the end of the wind.

"I will stop the wind," said the gruff old mountain. "I stand so high above the land the wind will have to stop."

But the wind blew higher and higher, up the side of the mountain, right over the top of the topmost rock on the top of the mountain, then rushed down through the forests on the other side.

And nothing could stop the wind.

"I will reach the end of the wind," said the airplane. "I will fly three times around the world, until I reach the end of the wind."

The airplane flew over mountains, over rivers, and over oceans, three times around the world, till it ran out of gas, but it never reached the end of the wind.

And the wind blew all over the world.

Finally, after days and days, when the wind grew tired of blowing and pushing birds and boats and clouds and kites, it sang another song:

*"Oh, I am the wind and I've been on a spree.*
*I've danced with the dandelions, ruffled the sea,*
*I've beaten an airplane and shaken a tree,*
*I did what I pleased, and they followed me!"*

Then the wind grew gentler and gentler and gentler and quietly rocked itself to sleep.

# THE GINGERBREAD BOY

## A Folk Tale
## retold by Gillian Kelly

here was once an old woman and man who had no child of their own and wanted one very much. One day the woman said to her husband, "I know what I shall do. I shall make us a nice gingerbread boy."

Her husband laughed at this idea, but the woman went right ahead and mixed up a batch of spicy brown dough. She rolled it out smooth and cut it neatly into the shape of a perfect little gingerbread boy.

With raisins for eyes, cinnamon candies for a mouth, and currant buttons marching down his coat, he was a fine sight indeed!

The woman popped him into the oven and waited for him to bake. When she thought he must be nearly done, she opened the oven door just to make sure. And in the wink of any eye the gingerbread boy hopped out of the oven and raced through the kitchen door and down the front path.

Flabbergasted, the woman ran out the door after him. "Come back, come back, gingerbread boy!" she called out. But he only laughed heartily and answered:

> *"Run, run, as fast as you can,*
> *You can't catch me,*
> *I'm the gingerbread man."*

And how right he was! The woman took off after him but could not catch up. Soon the two of them ran past her husband, who was busy at the woodpile. He threw down his axe and joined in on the chase.

But the gingerbread boy only laughed all the more when he saw the man. "I'm faster than the woman and faster than you," he said, and called out:

> *"Run, run, as fast as you can,*
> *You can't catch me,*
> *I'm the gingerbread man."*

Now, a fat little pig feeding at his trough looked up as the gingerbread boy ran past, and he thought how much better gingerbread would be than the same old slops. "Stop right here and give us a taste!" squealed the pig with delight.

But the gingerbread boy only raised his head and laughed.

"I'm faster than the woman and the old man, too. I'm faster than a fat little pig like you," he bellowed, and called out:

*"Run, run, as fast as you can,*
*You can't catch me,*
*I'm the gingerbread man."*

And the pig ran along as fast as his chubby little legs could carry him. How he wanted to eat that sweet little gingerbread boy! But he, too, was unable to catch up with the fleet little fellow, who skipped merrily into the meadow.

A speckled hare looked up from the clover he was busily nibbling at as the gingerbread boy streaked by. "Hmmm," he said. "I would like to nibble at you!"

But again the gingerbread boy laughed and said, "I'm faster than the woman and the old man, too. I'm faster than the pig, and I'm faster than you!" And again he called out:

> *"Run, run, as fast as you can,*
> *You can't catch me,*
> *I'm the gingerbread man."*

The rabbit hopped along behind as fast as he could go, but he could not keep up with the little gingerbread boy, who was running even faster now as he plunged into the woods.

The little gingerbread boy ran through the woods, and pretty soon he passed a black bear in a berry thicket. "Grrr!" growled the bear. "Stop right there. I'm going to gobble you up!"

But the gingerbread boy only laughed again and called out, "I'm faster than the woman and the old man, too . . . the pig and the rabbit, and faster than you!

> *"Run, run, as fast as you can,*
> *You can't catch me,*
> *I'm the gingerbread man."*

The bear lumbered along after the gingerbread boy all the same, but he could not catch up with him.

By now the gingerbread boy was feeling quite pleased with himself. He could run faster than anyone! He turned a cartwheel and called out at the top of his voice:

> *"Run, run, as fast as you can,*
> *You can't catch me,*
> *I'm the gingerbread man."*

Now, just at this moment a fox happened to be slinking by. When he saw the merry gingerbread boy, he, too, thought what a fine and tasty meal the boy would make. So he licked his chops and called out slyly, "What are you talking about? Catch you? Why would I want to catch a simple piece of gingerbread like you? I have better things to do with my time. Right now, for instance, I have to get across this river. Maybe you would like a ride to the other side? Hop on my tail!"

The gingerbread boy stopped and thought a moment. He looked back at the woman and the old man, at the pig and the hare and the bear. They were getting closer by the second and surely hungrier. And he looked down at his crisp little self and thought about getting wet—and *you* know what would happen to him then. So he accepted the fox's offer.

The gingerbread boy hopped onto the fox's tail, and they started across the river. After several minutes the fox said, "Little gingerbread boy, the current is swift. You had better

move onto my back, or you may fall off!"

So the gingerbread boy moved onto the fox's back.

The fox swam on farther yet, and soon he said, "Little gingerbread boy, the water is getting much deeper now. You would be wise to jump up onto my shoulder."

So the gingerbread boy jumped onto the fox's shoulder.

Soon the water got much, much deeper, and the fox said, "Hurry, hurry. The water is now very deep. I will hold my head up in the air and you can climb onto the tip of my nose."

So the gingerbread boy did just that.

But no sooner had he climbed onto the fox's nose than the fox whipped his head back, opened his mouth, and—*crunch, crunch, crunch!*—that was the end of the little gingerbread boy.

And this is the end of his tale.

# THE GOLDEN GOOSE

## by the Brothers Grimm
## retold by Sue Kassirer

here was once a man and a woman who had three sons. The youngest was named Simpleton, for people said that he was not very smart and could do not one thing right. Everyone laughed at him and ridiculed him to no end.

One day the eldest son decided to go into the forest to cut wood. As he was preparing to go, his mother gave him a rich, thick cake and a bottle of red wine to take along, so he would go neither hungry nor thirsty.

When he got to the forest, the son met a little old man who was all bent over and who walked with a cane.

The little old man tipped his hat, bade the son a good day, and said, "Give me a bit of that scrumptious cake you have there, and let me have a drop of that good red wine."

But the son was clever, for he said, "If I were to give you my cake and my wine, why, what should I have then for myself? So be off with you now."

And with that the boy left the man standing there and headed on his way.

But hardly had the boy even started to chop down a tree than his axe slipped and cut straight into his arm. He had no choice but to head home and have his wound tended to.

But mind you, this was no accident. This mishap was brought about by the workings of the little old man.

Now, the next day the second son headed into the forest to cut some wood. His mother packed him a rich sweet cake and a bottle of red wine, as she had done for his elder brother.

When the second son got to the forest, he was met by none other than the little old man. And the man said, "Please, lad, give me a piece of your fine cake and a drop of your wine."

But the second son was as clever as the first, and he responded, "If I give you some, then I will have less for myself. So be off with you now." With that, he left the old man standing there and headed on into the forest.

The second son's punishment was quickly issued, for no sooner had he given but a few blows to a tree than he hit his own leg and could barely hobble on home.

A few days later Simpleton said to his father, "Please, Father, let me go to the forest to cut us some wood."

But his father answered with, "Your wise brothers have already been harmed doing just that. Since you know nothing about wood cutting, it would be foolish for you to go."

Simpleton begged and pleaded, and at last his father said, "All right, go ahead, if that's what you want. Once you hurt yourself, you will become wiser."

And so Simpleton's mother packed him a cake as well. But unlike the cakes of his brothers, Simpleton's cake was mixed solely with water and had been baked in the ashes. And with it was packed only a bottle of sour beer.

But Simpleton was happy with what fare he had, and he headed off into the forest. He too was soon greeted by the little old man. "Give me some of the cake you carry and a drink of your red wine," said the man.

Simpleton answered, "I have merely a cake that has been baked in the ashes and some sour beer. But if such ordinary fare will please you, let's sit down and eat it together."

So they sat down to eat and drink together. And as Simpleton took out his plain cake it turned into a rich sweet cake, and as he took out the jug of sour beer it became a bottle of the finest wine. So they ate and they drank, and when they had finished the meal the little man turned to Simpleton and said, "Since you have shown me what a good heart you have, and since you have shared so willingly of your goods, I will now grant you good luck. See that tree over there? Chop it down, and you will find something very special at its roots." And with this, the old man swiftly disappeared.

So Simpleton chopped down the tree, and once it fell, what did he see sitting among the roots but a goose with feathers of pure gold. Simpleton lifted up the goose and took it with him to an inn where he had planned to spend the night.

Now, the innkeeper had three daughters who, on seeing the goose, grew quite excited and curious as to what kind of bird it could be. And each of them hankered for one of its golden feathers.

The eldest thought to herself, "If I wait patiently, surely there will be a moment when I can quickly pull out just one of those beautiful feathers." So when Simpleton had finally fallen asleep, she carefully reached out and grabbed one of the goose's wings, ready to pull out a golden feather. But her hand stuck fast to the wing. She pulled and tugged, yet she could not get away.

A little while later the second sister came along. She also

longed for a golden feather. But she didn't even get close to taking one. While speaking to her sister, she touched her sister's hand, and to her horror, the two stuck fast together.

At last the third sister came along with the same thing on her mind. How she wanted one of those golden feathers! The others cried out, "No, keep away, for goodness' sake—away!" But, she figured, if her sisters could gather around the rare golden goose, why couldn't she? So she moved toward the second sister, and she had barely touched her when, yes, she too became solidly stuck.

The three sisters all had to spend the night this way, stuck one to the other and finally to the goose.

The next morning Simpleton tucked the goose under his arm and headed on his way. He didn't notice the three girls stuck first to the goose and then to one another. They trailed on behind him like a loud and colorful banner, running first this way and then that, fussing and fighting and trying not to stumble over Simpleton's legs.

After some time this train of people ran into the parson, who on seeing the odd procession called out, "Shame on you, you young and naughty girls. Haven't your mothers taught you not to go running after a lad in such a way? Is this proper behavior?"

And he took hold of the hand of the youngest girl, meaning to pull her away. But as he touched her he found that he was stuck fast. And he, too, had to join the train and run along behind.

Shortly after, the sexton came along and, seeing his master following along on the heels of the three girls, called out in amazement, "Your Reverence! Your Reverence! To where do you run so fast? Have you forgotten that in one hour's time we have a christening?"

And so he ran after the parson, caught him by the sleeve, and was soon stuck as fast as the others.

As this party of five tramped on, one following on the heels of the other, they came upon two farmhands carrying hoes. The parson called to them and asked them to set the sexton and himself free. But the second they touched the sexton, they too were held fast. By now there were seven people running after Simpleton and his golden goose.

After some time this procession came to a town whose king had a daughter so solemn that no one but no one could make her laugh. The king had finally proclaimed that whoever could make the girl laugh would win her hand in marriage.

Simpleton had heard about this and decided to visit the princess. Soon he appeared with his goose and his train of seven people all running willy-nilly behind him (though of course he still did not know they were there). The princess took one look at this silly spectacle and burst into peals of laughter. It seemed she would never stop.

Thereupon Simpleton asked her to be his bride. But the king did not take well to Simpleton, and he tried to stop the marriage from happening. First he told Simpleton that he had to bring him a man who could drink up an entire cellarful of wine.

Simpleton thought at once of the little old man in the forest and how helpful he had been before. He went to look for him and found at the very spot where he had cut down the tree a very sad little man sitting on the tree stump.

Simpleton asked him what was wrong, and the man answered, "I am so very thirsty, but no matter how much I drink, it is not enough. Cold water is not to my liking, and I have already had an entire cask of wine. But what good is such a small drop as that on a burning stone?"

"Well, maybe I can help you out," said Simpleton. "If you come with me, you will soon have enough to drink and more."

Simpleton took the man to the king's cellar, and he began drinking from the great casks. He drank and he drank until it seemed he would surely burst. By the day's end the cellar was empty.

So again Simpleton went to the king and demanded his bride. But the king didn't like the idea of someone with a name like Simpleton marrying his daughter. So again he made a condition. He told Simpleton that he had to find a man who could eat a mountain of bread.

Without much thought Simpleton headed straight back to the forest. There on the same tree stump sat a very thin man who was tightening his belt and trying to make a new hole in the leather. And on his face was a pained expression.

"I have just eaten an ovenful of rolls," he moaned, "but what good is that to a man as frightfully hungry as I am? I eat and I eat, yet I am never satisfied. Every day I tighten my belt that much more and then fear I will die of hunger."

Simpleton was delighted to find such a man and said, "Come with me, then, and you shall finally have enough to eat."

So the man followed Simpleton to the court, where by the king's orders all the flour in the kingdom had been brought together and a towering mountain of bread baked. The hungry man from the forest sat down and began to eat . . . and eat . . . and eat, until, by the day's end, the mountain had disappeared.

Simpleton thought that surely now he could have his bride, but when he asked for the third time the king stammered and fumbled and tried to find an excuse. He finally asked for a ship that could sail not only on sea but on land as well.

"As soon as you sail up to my kingdom in such a vessel, you shall have my daughter's hand in marriage," said the king.

Simpleton headed straight for the forest, and there he found the little old man with whom he had shared his cake. And the little old man said, "I have eaten and drunk for you, and now I will give you the ship you need as well. I do all this for one reason and one reason only. I do it because you helped me when I was in need."

And so the old man gave Simpleton a most spectacular ship that could sail on land as well as on sea. When the king saw the ship, he could no longer think of any excuses for preventing the marriage. The wedding was glorious, and when the king died, Simpleton took the throne and lived a long and happy life with his wife, the queen.

# THE THREE BILLY GOATS GRUFF

## A Norwegian Folk Tale
## retold by Sue Kassirer

nce upon a time there were three billy goats, brothers named Gruff. There was Little Billy Goat Gruff, Middle Billy Goat Gruff, and Great Big Billy Goat Gruff.

They lived on the side of a mountain, where day after day they munched happily on fresh green grass.

Now, one day the goats found that there was not one blade of grass left on the side of the mountain. They had eaten it all up! So they decided to visit the big green meadow on the other side of the stream and on up the hill.

To cross the stream the billy goats Gruff had to walk over a creaky wooden bridge. And under this bridge lived an old troll with great goggle eyes and an ugly crooked nose as long as your arm!

Rumor had it that the troll didn't want *any*one using his bridge and that he loved nothing better than to eat billy goats. So of course most billy goats never even thought of going over the bridge. And that was why the grass in the meadow was so long and thick and green.

As the days passed the three billy goats Gruff grew leaner and leaner and hungrier and hungrier. They finally became so hungry that they decided they had to cross the bridge.

So the next day the three billy goats set out for the meadow. Little Billy Goat Gruff led the way. *Trip-trap, trip-trap, trip-trap.* He was so small and light that his teeny little hoofs made only a small sound as he trip-trapped over the wooden bridge.

"*Who* is tripping over my bridge?" roared a voice that made the bridge tremble as it creaked. It was the voice of the troll, whose sharp, pointy ears heard *everything.* Little Billy Goat Gruff nearly fell from fright.

But instead he called out, "It is I, Little Billy Goat Gruff, on my way to the big green meadow for a bite to eat. Good day, sir." And he lifted his hoof, ready to continue tripping over the bridge.

"Eat? *You* eat?" bellowed the troll, and he laughed so hard the bridge now shook wildly. "*I'm* the one who is going to eat. I'm going to eat *you*—right up! I love billy goats!"

"Oh, no, please!" begged Little Billy Goat Gruff. "You can't see me, but I am so teeny that I'd hardly make a mouthful.

You would do much better to eat my middle brother. He happens to be on his way over here right now."

The troll grunted and grumbled, since he didn't like to wait for anything—least of all a good meal. But he liked a full meal, too, so he let Little Billy Goat Gruff go on his way and waited for Middle Billy Goat Gruff to come along.

*Trip-trap, trip-trap, trip-trap.* It wasn't long before Middle Billy Goat Gruff's medium-sized hoofs came trip-trapping over the wooden bridge.

"Who is *that* trip-trapping over my bridge?" roared the troll again in a voice even deeper than before.

"It's just I, Middle Billy Goat Gruff," answered the goat in a loud, clear voice. "I'm on my way to the big green meadow, and when I get there I will eat and eat until I become big and round and fat."

"That's what you think!" said the troll, and he laughed fiendishly. "Forget your green meadow! I'm going to eat you up!"

"Oh, please don't do such a foolish thing!" begged the middle-size goat. "If you wait just a moment or two, my big brother will be right along. Surely you'd rather eat him. He'll make a much grander meal than I."

Now, the troll was a greedy fellow, and the bigger the meal the better, so he growled, "Off with you, then. Skedaddle!"

So Middle Billy Goat Gruff briskly scampered off to the big green meadow, where he joined his younger brother.

A few minutes later Great Big Billy Goat Gruff came stomping along. *TRIP-TRAP, TRIP-TRAP, TRIP-TRAP* went his heavy hoofs as he marched over the wooden bridge. The sound echoed far and wide.

"*Whooo* is tramping over my bridge?" roared the troll. His voice was deafening by now, and an easy match for Great Big Billy Goat's thundering hoofs.

"*It is I, the very biggest Billy Goat Gruff,*" bellowed Great Big Billy Goat Gruff in a voice that made the trees fling up their boughs for mercy.

"Ah, you! I've been waiting for you! I'm going to eat you up!" said the troll. And he licked his chops and lifted himself over the side of the bridge. There he crouched, with his great goggle eyes and his ugly crooked nose that was as long as your arm. And he headed straight for Great Big Billy Goat Gruff. He couldn't wait to eat him!

But Great Big Billy Goat Gruff just lowered his head, fixed his eyes on the troll, aimed his great curling horns right at him, and butted. The troll went flying, flying. . . . He flew straight off the wooden bridge, high into the air, and then on

into the rushing stream. And it is said that he has never been heard from since.

So Great Big Billy Goat Gruff tripped on to the big green meadow, where he joined his brothers, who were already happily munching on the luscious green grass, which was even fresher and taller than any of them had imagined it could be.

The three goats feasted until they could eat no more, and became so fat that they had to waddle home, back over the creaky bridge.

And the last that was heard, the three Gruff brothers were still the plumpest and fattest goats for miles around.

*Snip, snap, snout,*
*Now this story's out.*

# THE LITTLE SNOW MAIDEN

## A Russian Folk Tale
## retold by Sue Kassirer

nce upon a time, far, far away, there lived an old man and an old woman named Peter and Anna. They were good people and happy but for one thing. They had never had any children of their own. And they longed deeply for just one child.

Every day Peter and Anna would stand by their window and watch the neighbors' children laughing and playing outdoors. And more than once they would wish with all their hearts that one of these children was their own.

One winter day as Peter and Anna watched, the children built a large snow fort and pelted one another playfully with snowballs. And once they tired of the snowball war, the children began to build a huge snowman. They rolled the snow into three large balls, each a little smaller than the last, and piled them one on top of the other. They finished the snowman off with sticks for arms, a carrot for a nose, acorns for eyes, and large juicy raisins for a mouth.

As Peter watched the children building the snowman, he had an idea. "Why don't we make ourselves a little snow girl?" he said, turning anxiously to Anna. "Who knows, maybe she'll come to life and become the daughter we have so longed for."

"Why not, " said Anna with a shrug. "We have nothing to lose by doing so."

And so the two of them put on their heavy winter coats, donned their warm fur caps, and headed for their backyard, where they could work undisturbed by their neighbors.

Together the couple rolled the snow, packed it, and gradually formed it into the shape of a little maiden. And so lovely and beautiful was she that it was clear that such beauty could only have come from Peter and Anna's years of tenderly and lovingly dreaming of a child of their own.

It was not until early evening, when the neighborhood children's laughter had ceased echoing over the hills, the sound of dinner preparations had ceased, and the sky had taken on the shade of a smoky opal that the snow maiden was finally finished. She stood before Peter and Anna, incredible and complete.

"Just look at her!" cried Peter with delight. "If only she would now speak to us or give us some sign of life!"

"Yes, run and play as the other children do," pleaded Anna. And she looked straight into the eyes of the snow maiden and wished ever so strongly that the icy form before her would give some sign that it was more than a block of snow.

And suddenly, as if by magic, the eyelids of the snow creature began to quiver ever so slightly, her lips began to curl slowly, slowly upward into what could only be called a smile, and her stark white cheeks took on a rosy flush. But it was only when her eyes opened wide that Peter and Anna knew their wish had come true. The snow maiden was alive!

As she came more fully to life the snow maiden began to dance around, twirling about and laughing softly as snowflakes fell on her face, her hands, her arms . . . and comfortably blended right in.

"Thanks be to the heavens!" Peter cried out. "Our wish has been met, our longing satisfied. We have a daughter all our own!"

Anna ran inside and grabbed a warm blanket, which she and Peter wrapped snugly around the shoulders of the little snow maiden, so to keep her warm. And Peter picked her up and carried her into the house.

At this, the snow maiden spoke her first words. "Please," she said in a silvery voice, "I must not be kept too warm. Over there by the window would be just fine."

Peter placed her carefully on a chair near the window, far from the hot stove. And the snow maiden looked up at him with a smile that clearly held a daughter's love.

Anna went to the closet and brought out a small white fur coat that had once been her own, and Peter went to a neighbor's house and borrowed a little fur hat and a pair of soft white leather boots with fur around the rims.

Once she was dressed, the little snow maiden jumped up, moved toward the door, and exclaimed, "Oh, it is stifling hot here in the cottage. I must go outside and cool off!"

"But my dear child, it's time you had some proper rest," said Anna. "Come, dear one. I'll tuck you into bed."

"Oh, no, not me!" cried the snow maiden, and she looked quite horrified. "I am a maiden of the snow. I cannot be put under warm covers or tucked in a bed. Instead, I must dance

and play in the yard all night." And with that, the snow maiden danced out the door into the cold of the winter's night. She was quite a sight to behold. Her garments moved and glistened in the moonlight, and the frost settled about her golden head and shone like a crown of sparkling jewels.

Peter and Anna stood by the window and watched the snow maiden for hours. Again and again they said, "How thankful we are, thankful beyond words, for the precious little girl who has come to us." And although they did finally go to bed, they arose time and time again throughout the night to look outside and make sure that their precious dear had not run away or, worse yet, been merely a dream. But each time they looked, there she was, still dancing merrily, alone in the moonlight.

In the morning the snow maiden ran into the kitchen, her blue eyes shining with delight. In her hands was a small piece of ice. "This is my porridge," she announced, and showed Anna how to crush it in a wooden bowl. That was all the snow maiden would ever eat.

After breakfast the snow maiden ran outdoors and played with the other children. How they loved her! She was full of spirit and energy—and could run faster than all the others. As she ran, her eyes twinkled and gleamed in the sunlight. And her laugh was like the sound of tiny silver bells.

Peter and Anna watched her with great pride.

"She is really ours. All our own!" said Anna.

"Our dear little daughter," said Peter.

When she was hungry, the snow maiden came inside for her ice porridge. And although Anna said to her, "Surely you wish to sleep inside tonight, my darling," the answer was as it had been before: "Oh, no, not me. I am a maiden of the snow."

And so it went all through the winter. Peter and Anna had never dreamed of such happiness. The snow maiden was forever singing and laughing and dancing, in and out of the house, back and forth, back and forth. And she was a generous and willing girl, doing everything Anna asked of her in good spirit and without complaint. But she would never, but never, sleep indoors. The snow maiden was most content, happy, and comfortable when surrounded by cool breezes and swirling snowflakes. And no storm was ever too harsh. The more severe the storm, the more at peace the snow maiden grew.

But there came the day when the first signs of spring began to show themselves. The snow started to melt, and tiny crocus shoots pushed their way up through the thawing ground. At the same time, the snow maiden began to droop and appeared to be longing strongly for something. She grew wistful and sad.

One day she said to Peter and Anna:

> *"The time has come when I must go*
> *To join my friends, Frost and Snow.*
> *Good-bye, my dears, my dears, good-bye.*
> *Back I go across the sky!"*

Peter and Anna wept loudly and pleaded with the snow maiden. They wanted to keep her all to themselves and share her with no one.

"But you mustn't go, our dear one, you mustn't!" cried Peter.

"You cannot go, you cannot leave us!" cried Anna.

And while Peter ran to the door and barred it, Anna threw her arms lovingly but forcefully around the snow maiden and held her close.

"You mustn't leave us! We won't let you go! You mustn't!" they both cried. But even as Anna held her ever so tightly, the snow maiden began to melt slowly away in her arms. And finally there was nothing left of the maiden but a pool of water by the stove with the little fur hat sitting in it, the small fur coat, and the pair of white leather boots. Yet Peter and Anna felt, as they gazed at the spot where the maiden had been, that she still stood there before them, with her blue eyes shining and her golden hair streaming. And faintly, faintly, they thought they could still hear her singing:

*"The time has come when I must go*
*To join my friends, Frost and Snow.*
*Good-bye, my dears, my dears, good-bye.*
*Back I go across the sky!"*

85

"No! Please stay! Stay!" Peter and Anna begged her, reaching out as if they could grab the image they thought they saw before them. But all at once the door that Peter had barred burst open with a force like none either of them had ever seen before. An icy wind ripped into the room and swirled wildly around. And although Peter quickly shut the door once again, it was to no use. The snow maiden was gone. She had vanished altogether.

Peter and Anna wept and wept, for they were sure that now they would never again see the snow maiden. Anna carefully put away the clothing that had been left behind. But often throughout the hot summer months she could not help but take out the fur hat, the little coat, and the white leather boots and kiss them as she thought of her dear snow maiden.

One starlit night when winter had come again, Peter and Anna were awakened by a familiar silvery peal of laughter. Could it be? It seemed too good to be true!

"Doesn't that sound just like our little snow maiden?" Peter asked breathlessly as he ran to open the door. And sure enough,

there she was! The snow maiden danced into the room, and as she danced she sang:

> *"By winter night and winter day*
> *Your love calls me here to stay.*
> *Here till spring I'll stay and then*
> *I'm back to Frost and Snow again."*

Peter and Anna held the snow maiden tightly, then handed her her pretty white clothes. She soon ran out to the gleaming snow, tripping down the moonlight's silver path, her clothing glittering like diamonds. And the frost again settled about her golden head like a crown of sparkling jewels.

And each year at springtime, off the snow maiden headed to the North to frolic through the summer with her friends Frost and Snow up on the frozen seas. And with time Peter and Anna came not to mind her leaving so much, for they knew that every year, with the falling of the leaves, would come the return of their darling, the snow maiden.

# THE BREMEN TOWN MUSICIANS

## by Walter de la Mare
## retold by Deborah Hautzig

nce upon a time there was a poor old donkey. For eighteen years he worked hard carrying meal for his master, the miller. Now he was nothing more than a bag of bones.

One cold frosty night as he stood close to the mill for warmth, he heard the miller say to his wife, "The old donkey must go. He's been a good servant, but now he's old and slow. He doesn't earn his keep. He's not worth more than his skin!"

"Well, then," said his wife, "we'll skin him tomorrow and sell the skin!"

The donkey shivered with fear, and his knobby old knees shook under him. But he knew what he had to do: he had to leave at once.

"Whatever happens to me now, it surely can't be worse than a skinning," he said to himself. And so the donkey sneaked off and began walking down the road that led to Bremen.

A little after daybreak the donkey came to an ancient stone cross. And stretched out beneath it lay an old hound dog. The hound told the donkey that he had run away from his master.

"My master was a hunter," said the hound. "I served him loyally all my life. But two days ago I heard him say I was old and my scent was gone. He said all I was good for was to make cat's food out of me!"

"I am in the same situation myself," said the donkey kindly. "But I can still bray a little, and I am sure you could howl quite well if you needed to. Come with me to Bremen. We can join the town band. They are fine musicians, and I am sure they will welcome us."

So they went on together. They had not gone more than a mile or two when they saw an old gray tabby cat. She was sitting on an orchard wall in the sun, and her face was as sad as a rainy day in December.

"Good morning, cat," said the donkey. "You're not looking very chipper this day."

"Chipper?" said the cat. "You wouldn't either, if you were me! The minute my mistress catches me, she going to *drown* me!"

"But *why*?" asked the hound.

"Because I am old and worn out. I spent my whole life catching mice for her. Night after night I have kept her company, purred and played games with her. I've shown her every affection. But she has no pity, no mercy. I will be drowned tomorrow."

"All humans are like that," mumbled the old hound.

"Most, but not all," said the donkey. "Listen, dear cat. My friend and I have a plan. We are off to Bremen to join the town band. I bet you can still strike up a tune or two when the moon is full! Come with us. I am sure the good people of Bremen will be thrilled to have the three of us in their band!"

So the three old creatures went on together. The miles went by slowly. By and by they came to a tumble-down shed near a duck pond. Perched on the roof of the shed was an old rooster. He was so ruffled and woebegone he looked even sadder than the cat.

The donkey politely asked him the way to Bremen, and the rooster said they had five more miles to go.

"As for me," said the rooster, "I want to go to a better world. My master, the farmer, says I'm no use to him now, though I have protected his hens and eggs for years. Not a night has passed, summer or winter, without my warning him that it was nearly time to get up. Nobody dares enter the farmyard while *I* guard it. But it's all forgotten! He has no mercy. He will wring my neck tomorrow and boil me for supper!"

"All humans are like that," said the hound.

"Most, but not all," said the donkey. "And I'll bet, Mr. Rooster, that you can still yell cock-a-doodle when the sun comes up!"

"Indeed I can," said the rooster, standing up a bit straighter. He preened, flapped his sheeny wings, and crowed softly so the farmer wouldn't hear him, "Cock-a-doodle-dooo!"

"Bravo, friend!" said the donkey. "An excellent note. You *must* come with us. We are all off to Bremen to join the town band. One is one, two is two, three is three—but four is a quartet!"

So off they went together. But all four were tired and hungry and in a strange place, and before long they lost their way. To make matters even worse, nighttime came, and it was bitter cold.

"How will we ever find shelter for the night?" asked the hound.

After they talked things over, the rooster flew high up into a fir tree. "I see a twinkling light!" called the rooster. "Let's go see what it is." He flew down and led his friends through the dark woods.

Soon they came to a fine stone house beside a stream. A bright light was shining in its windows. The four friends whispered to one another in the dark. At last the old cat crept up to the window sill and peeked in.

When the cat came back, she told her friends what she had seen. "There's a great feast going on. There's a blazing fire and a table heaped with wonderful food." Everyone was very hungry, and their mouths watered as the cat told them of the many pies and sweetmeats, breads, and wines. "And," said the cat, "they must be robbers. The tables and chairs are piled with gold and silver, and there is a huge bag of money on the floor. I've never seen anything like it!"

"Mmm," said the donkey. "I could munch a few loaves of bread right now."

The hound's mouth watered as he thought of the sweet-meats.

The cat's whiskers twitched at the memory of rich cream and broiled fish.

The rooster longed for a piece of pie.

He had an idea. "Let's make some music for them. Perhaps even robbers have hearts and will give us some supper."

So the four friends crept over to the window. The hound leaped onto the donkey's back. The cat jumped up and sat on the hound's back. The rooster flew up and perched on the cat's back. Then all at once they burst into song.

*"Aaaaaaaah!"* screamed the robbers, jumping out of their seats in terror. To them the sudden noise of the animals' voices sounded like the shriek of demons! The robbers ran out of the house so fast they knocked over all the lights.

"Hurray!" shouted the four friends. They went into the house, sat together merrily at the table, and had a huge feast.

After supper, they said good night to one another. The donkey found a cozy bed on some bundles of straw in the yard. The hound lay down behind the door. The cat curled up in the warm ashes from the fire. The rooster flew up onto the curtain rod to roost until morning. Each one was full and happy and warm, and soon all four were fast asleep.

Meanwhile, the robbers were hiding in the woods nearby, working up the courage to go back to the house. They wanted to get their loot. Around midnight the house was dark and all was still. The captain of the robbers told one of his men to go back into the house to see what he could find.

Quaking with fear, the robber crawled through an open window. It was pitch dark, except for the two shining eyes of the cat.

The robber thought those shining eyes were coals smoldering in the fire. "Good, I can light a candle," he said to himself, stooping down and poking his candle right in the cat's eye!

The cat yowled with fury, spitting and scratching at the robber. She leaped right into his face!

Scared out of his wits, the robber ran to the door. *Crash!* He tripped over the hound. The hound sprang up. He bared the few teeth he had left and bit the robber on the leg!

The robber limped frantically across the dark yard and into the straw. What a surprise he had! He fell right over the donkey, who gave him a swift kick with his hoof.

By now the rooster was awake from all the noise. He flew down from the curtain rod and yelled at the robber as he had never yelled before.

The robber fled back to his captain. "There's a witch in the house!" he cried. "She spat at me and scratched me with her talons. By the door was an assassin with a knife. He stabbed me in the leg! In the yard there's a horrible four-handed monster who beat me with a club. Then a screaming demon came out of the clouds and chased me. Hurry! We must escape while there's still time!"

Well, the robbers never went near *that* house again. The four friends were so snug and happy in the house, they decided not to go to Bremen just yet. Instead they stayed in the stone house by the stream and practiced their singing. Every morning and every evening they sang, and they made lovely music together. A finer quartet has never been heard.

# THE LITTLE RED HEN

## An English Folk Tale
## retold by Gillian Kelly

here was once a little red hen who had five chicks. One spring day, while pecking around the farmyard, she came across a fat little grain of wheat.

"Who will help me plant this wheat?" asked the Little Red Hen.

"Not I," honked the goose.

"Not I," quacked the duck.

"Not I," bleated the lamb.

"All right, then," said the Little Red Hen as she preened her feathers. "I'll just plant it myself."

And she did.

After a while the wheat came up, tall and golden. When it could grow no higher and was ready to be cut, the Little Red Hen called out, "Now, who will help me harvest this golden wheat?"

"Not I," honked the goose.

"Not I," quacked the duck.

"Not I," bleated the lamb.

"Well, then, I guess I'll just have to harvest it myself," said the Little Red Hen.

And she did.

Once the wheat was all harvested, the Little Red Hen needed to take the grain from its husk. "Who will help me thresh this wheat?" she asked the other barnyard animals.

"Not I," honked the goose.

"Not I," quacked the duck.

"Not I," bleated the lamb.

"Well, well, now," said the Little Red Hen. "I'll just go and thresh it myself."

And she did.

Soon the wheat was all threshed, and the Little Red Hen needed to carry it to the old stone mill to have it ground into a fine flour.

"Who will help me carry this grain to the stone mill?" clucked the Little Red Hen.

"Not I," honked the goose.

"Not I," quacked the duck.

"Not I," bleated the lamb.

"Well, in that case, I'll just pick it up and carry it there myself," said the Little Red Hen.

And she did.

Once the wheat was ground into a fine flour, the Little Red Hen was ready to make it into a loaf of bread.

"Who will help me make this fine flour into a loaf of the freshest bread?" asked the Little Red Hen.

"Not I," honked the goose.

"Not I," quacked the duck.

"Not I," bleated the lamb.

"Ah, very well, then," said the Little Red Hen. "I guess I'll just bake a loaf of bread myself."

And she did.

When the loaf was baked, the Little Red Hen carried it hot and steaming and ever so fragrant from the oven to the table.

"Now, who will come and help me eat this hot fresh bread?" clucked the Little Red Hen.

"Oh, *I* will, of course!" honked the goose.

"And so will I!" quacked the duck.

"And don't forget me—I will too!" bleated the lamb.

"Oh, no, you won't! Not one of you!" said the Little Red Hen. "For who planted the seed, who harvested and threshed the wheat, who carried it to the stone mill to have it ground into flour, and who baked the tasty loaf you are now so hungrily eyeing?"

"You did," honked the goose.

"You did," quacked the duck.

"You did," bleated the lamb.

"That's right," said the Little Red Hen. "*I* did. And I will share it with none other than my chicks."

And she did!

# THE HARE
# AND THE HEDGEHOG

## by Walter de la Mare
## retold by Deborah Hautzig

arly one Sunday morning, when the cowslips were budding and the lilacs were in bloom, a hedgehog came to his little door to look out at the weather. It was a fine clear day.

"I think I'll take a little walk into the fields to see how our nettle plants are doing," the hedgehog told his wife.

Off went the hedgehog, whistling as he stepped along. As he came around a blackberry bush he met a hare who was out looking at his spring cabbages.

The hedgehog smiled politely and said, "Good morning."

The hare, who thought quite a lot of himself, sneered at the hedgehog. "What are *you* doing out so early?" he said.

"I'm taking a walk," replied the hedgehog.

"A walk?" said the hare with a sniff. "Surely you can find something better to do with those crooked legs of yours!"

This made the hedgehog very angry. It was bad enough that nature had given him crooked legs—he couldn't bear to have nasty things said about them. He bristled and said, "You seem to think you can do more with your legs than I can with mine."

"Perhaps," said the hare airily.

100

"Well, I say you *can't*," said the hedgehog. "Start fair, and I'll beat you in a race every time!"

"A race, dear Mr. Hedgehog?" said the hare. "You must be joking. It's so ridiculous! Still, what will you bet?"

"I'll bet a gold coin to a bottle of brandy," said the hedgehog.

"Done!" said the hare. "Shake hands, and we'll start at once."

"Not so fast," said the hedgehog. "I've had no breakfast yet! I will meet you here in half an hour." The hare agreed and took a frisky practice run while the hedgehog went shuffling home.

When he arrived, he said to his wife, "My dear, I need your help. Come with me at once into the field."

"Why, what's going on?" she said.

"I have bet the hare a gold coin to a bottle of brandy that I'll beat him in a race. You must come and see it."

"Oy, vey!" cried Mrs. Hedgehog. "Have you gone crazy? You! Run a race with a hare!"

"Calm down, dear. I have a plan," said Mr. Hedgehog. "I'll tell you about it when we get there."

When the hedgehogs came to the plowed field, Mr. Hedgehog said to his wife, "Listen carefully, my dear. The hare is on the other end of the field. He and I will start the race over there in these furrows. But as soon as I have gone a few inches and he can't see me, I will turn back."

"Then what?" said Mrs. Hedgehog.

"Then you must pretend to be me! When the hare comes out of his furrow on this end, you will be sitting here huffing and puffing. When you see him you will say, 'Aha! So you've come at last!' "

Mrs. Hedgehog smiled at her husband and said, "You are so clever! I will gladly do what you said."

So the hedgehog went to the meet the hare.

"How shall we run?" asked the hare scornfully. "Down or over, sideways or longways—it's all the same to me."

"Well, let's see," said the hedgehog. "I have watched you run with your friends many times, and you run very well. But you never keep straight. You all run around and around in circles, playing and chasing each other as if you were crazy. But you can't run a race like that. You must run in a straight line."

"I *know* that," said the hare angrily.

"Very well," said the hedgehog. "You run in that furrow, and I'll run in this one."

The hare, who was quicker on his feet than in his wits, agreed. "One, two, three—*go!*" he shouted, and off he went like a whirlwind across the field. But the hedgehog, after scuttling along a few inches, turned back and sat still.

When the hare came out of his furrow at the other end of the field, Mrs. Hedgehog sat there panting as if she would never catch her breath. She looked exactly like her husband.

"Aha! So you've come at last?" she said.

The hare was shocked. His ears trembled, and his eyes bulged.

"You've run it! You've run it!" he cried in astonishment.

"Yes," said Mrs. Hedgehog. "I was afraid you had gone lame."

"Lame?" said the hare. "Lame, indeed! But after all, what's one furrow? You said you'd beat me every time. We'll try again."

The hare was off and running again, and he ran faster than ever. But when he came out of his furrow at the other end, there was Mr. Hedgehog!

The hedgehog laughed, and said, "Aha! So you are here again—at last!"

The hare was so enraged he could hardly speak. "Twice is not enough! Make it three for luck. Let's run again!"

"As many times as you want, dear friend," said the hedge-hog. "It's the long run that really counts."

Again and again the hare raced up and down the long fur-row of the field, and every time he reached one end, and then the other, there was the hedgehog saying, "Aha! So here you are again—at last!"

Finally the hare couldn't run anymore. He lay on the grass panting and speechless. He looked pathetic, his fur bedraggled and his eyes dim.

Mrs. Hedgehog went off to the hare's house to get the bot-tle of brandy.

News of the race spread far and wide, and from that day to this, there has never been a race to compare with it.

# Goldilocks and the Three Bears

## retold by Gillian Kelly

here were once three bears who lived together in a little house in the woods. There was great big Papa Bear, medium-size Mama Bear, and teeny tiny Baby Bear.

One morning Mama Bear cooked up a steaming-hot batch of porridge. She poured a great big serving into Papa Bear's bowl, a medium-size serving into her own bowl, and a teeny tiny serving into Baby Bear's bowl.

But the porridge was much too hot to eat right away, so the three bears headed off for a walk in the woods while it cooled.

Now, at that very moment a little girl with long golden braids was also taking a walk in the woods. Her name was Goldilocks. As she walked she came to the house of the three bears. Goldilocks knocked on the door, and when there was no answer she decided to walk right in!

The first thing Goldilocks saw was the three bowls of steaming-hot porridge. She was very hungry, for her walk had been a long one. So she decided to take just a little taste.

First Goldilocks tried the porridge in Papa Bear's big bowl. "Ooh!" she said, dropping the spoon. "This porridge is much too hot for me."

Then she tried the porridge in Mama Bear's medium-size bowl. "Brrrr," she said, making a face. "This porridge is much too cold for me."

And finally she tried the porridge in Baby Bear's teeny tiny bowl. "Ah," she said with a smile. "This porridge is just right!" And she ate it all up.

Then Goldilocks walked into the living room and found a great big chair, which was Papa Bear's chair. She climbed up onto it but quickly climbed back down again. "This chair is much too big for me," she said as she slid down to the floor.

So she then climbed up onto Mama Bear's medium-size chair but just as quickly climbed down from this one, saying, "This one is much too hard for me."

Finally she tried Baby Bear's teeny tiny chair and was quite pleased with how well she fit, when—*crunch!*—it cracked and fell all to pieces.

After Goldilocks had gotten herself up again, she yawned and decided to take a nap. So she went upstairs and found the bears' bedroom. First she climbed up onto Papa Bear's bed. "This is much too high for me," she said as she peered way down at the floor far below.

Next she tried Mama Bear's bed, but it was much too soft.

So finally she tried Baby Bear's teeny tiny bed, which was neither too high nor too soft. "This bed is just right for me," she said, and she snuggled under the covers and fell fast asleep.

Not long after that the three bears headed home, for they were hungry and wanted to eat their cooled-off porridge. As soon as they walked in the door, they could see that someone had been in their house.

*"Someone has been eating my porridge,"* said Papa Bear in a great booming voice.

"And someone has been eating *my* porridge," said Mama Bear in her medium-size voice.

"And someone has been eating *my* porridge," squeaked Baby Bear in his teeny tiny baby voice. "And they have eaten it all up!"

So the three bears decided to sit down and think about this. First Papa Bear went to his great big chair and saw that the cushion was not as straight as he always left it. *"Someone has been sitting in my chair,"* he bellowed in an even bigger Papa Bear voice than usual.

Then Mama Bear went to her medium-size chair and saw that the cushion was all squashed down. "And someone has been sitting in *my* chair," she added in her medium-size Mama Bear voice.

And finally Baby Bear went to his teeny tiny chair, and he let out a shriek. "Someone has been sitting in *my* chair," he cried, "and they've broken it all to pieces!"

By now the three bears were quite worried and thought they had better look upstairs as well.

So great big Papa Bear went to look at his bed and saw that the pillow had been knocked down onto the floor. *"Someone has been sleeping in my bed,"* he thundered in his great big Papa Bear voice.

And Mama Bear saw that the cover on her bed had been partly turned down. "And someone has been sleeping in *my* bed," she added in her medium-size Mama Bear voice.

But most surprised of all was teeny tiny Baby Bear, who piped up in his teeny tiny Baby Bear voice. "And someone has been sleeping in *my* bed, and here she is!"

Just at that moment Goldilocks woke up out of a deep sleep, and when she saw the great big Papa Bear and the medium-size Mama Bear and the teeny tiny Baby Bear all standing by the bed staring down at her, she leaped out of the bed and bounded straight through the window to the ground below.

Now, she must not have hurt herself, for she got up quickly and ran . . . and ran . . . all the way home, faster than she had ever run before, and never saw the three bears again.

And as for the bears, they fixed up their home and went about their lives just as they had before. But every so often they thought of the little girl with the long golden braids and how quickly she had leaped from the bed to the window and off through the woods, never to be seen again.

# THE MAN
# WHO HAD NO DREAM

## by Adelaide Holl

r. Oliver was the richest man in town.

All day long he sat at his window and watched everyone else work hard for a living. Mr. Oliver didn't have to work. He had so much money he could buy anything he wanted.

Every evening Mr. Oliver sat at his window and waited for people to come home from work. Tired after a busy day, the townsfolk rested and looked out at the stars and the moon and the night. But not for long. They were too yawny and drowsy and sleepy from working so hard.

Soon they all went to bed and fell fast asleep. After a while, Mr. Oliver went to bed, too. But he didn't fall fast asleep. He just lay tossing and turning on his fine bed.

The weary workers quickly drifted off to the land of dreams.

They dreamed happy dreams made of wishes and hopes. They dreamed unhappy dreams made of fears and tears.

But Mr. Oliver couldn't sleep because he wasn't tired. And he couldn't dream because he had nothing to dream about— no wishes, no hopes, no fears, no tears.

## THE MAN WHO HAD NO DREAM

Night after night, he tried sleeping in different beds—each one more beautiful than the last.

Night after night, he walked back and forth, back and forth. Still he couldn't sleep, and he couldn't dream. He just waited for morning to come so he could go back to his window and watch everyone else work hard for a living.

One night, when Mr. Oliver was very wide awake and very much alone, he heard a noise at his window. He went to look. He found a little hurt bird that had fluttered and fallen on his windowsill.

"Poor little thing," Mr. Oliver said sadly. "The city is no place for birds."

He lifted the little bird very gently and carried it inside. He put it to bed on a silk cushion. He fed it milk from a silver spoon. Carefully he bandaged its hurt wing.

Mr. Oliver worked and worked. At last—tired and yawny and drowsy and sleepy—he fell asleep with the little bird in his arms. And while Mr. Oliver slept, something quite wonderful happened.

Mr. Oliver began to dream!

He dreamed there was a place in the city meant just for birds. He dreamed about a park for birds—with flowers and birdbaths and trees.

The next morning, bright and early, Mr. Oliver hurried outdoors, and for the first time in his life, he began to work. He spaded and raked and planted and watered. He built a beautiful park all planted with leafy trees and bright flowers. People and laughing children came there to romp and play and picnic on the grassy hills.

From that day on, Mr. Oliver never had trouble going to sleep. And he never slept without a dream. Mr. Oliver was a happy, busy man—a man with wishes and hopes and fears and tears.

# THE DREAMING BUNNY

## by Margaret Wise Brown

nce there was a bunny who liked only the very early morning. He loved the first rays of the round sun square on his nose. He loved the frost that made the world look like the dream he had just been having of a glass forest. Early in the morning the big leaves of the sassafras were etched in white—the blades of grass shiny and brittle with ice and the feathery flowering grasses glassy and sparkling like diamonds. So in some magic way the little bunny felt still a part of his dreams in the morning.

But later, when the rays of the big round sun fell on the treetops and the mother bunnies began calling their babies to help them wash up, then, oh, then the little bunny would go and hide in the immense folding leaves of a cabbage. He was so little he could sit inside a cabbage and peek out through the immense folding leaves.

And because he went on like this he was called the Bunny No Good.

When the other little bunnies were hopping about doing their work, there was the Bunny No Good sitting in a cabbage.

But, do you know, he never missed a thing.

He wasn't really sleeping, he was just a dreamy bunny.

And his little red ruby eyes blinked out of his square fur face and they never missed a trick. He saw the spiders spin their webs and he watched the foolish flies fly into them. He saw the mole start down a long hole to go off far down his tunnel and dig under someone's flat green lawn. He saw the other rabbits jumping about and running in circles, and he knew all their funny little wiggles. The way they twitched their whiskers, the way they kicked sideways and wiggled their noses and thumped the earth with their hind legs when they were startled. And he made a dreamy little song to himself about rabbits:

> *"Whiskers whisk,*
> *Twitch, twitch the nose.*
> *So red the eye, a ruby glows.*
> *Shinier than a wet red rose*
> *In a rabbit's face.*
> *Grow, grow.*
> *Eat and grow.*
> *What for*
> *Rabbits never know."*

All this time there was another little rabbit who went hopping about bright as a button, merry as a cricket, fit as a fiddle, busy as a beaver, and keen as a whistle.

His name was Bunny Bun Bun. And his big fat mother looked down her soft fur face and said to the other eleven hundred little rabbits, "Look at Bunny Bun Bun. If you all want to be bright as a button, merry as a cricket, fit as a fiddle, busy as a beaver, and keen as a whistle, just do as Bunny Bun Bun does."

All this time the Bunny No Good was singing and dreaming and blinking away to himself in the immense folding leaves of a cabbage.

He watched a flock of wild black crows go flying through the sky screaming their awful wild-crow music.

He watched them light in an old fat oak tree, making a crown of crows on the topmost branches.

All this was still very early in the morning.

Some of the frost had been melted into shiny wet water by the sun. Where the trees cast their shadows there was a shadow of frost on the ground, a white shadow away from the sun, a white triangle shadow for the pine trees and the holly bushes and a great spreading feathery shadow for the other trees.

All this the Bunny No Good noticed as he dreamed away the bright early morning minutes in his cabbage.

But not Bunny Bun Bun and the eleven hundred other little scurrying rabbits. They were too busy bustling about washing and dusting and making little straw bunny beds and sweeping and polishing and peeling carrots for lunch.

They did not notice the shadow of frost beneath the trees or the crown of crows in the old oak at the edge of the wood. They did not listen to the wild-crow music. They were too busy about their own little bunny business.

And so they did not notice that the crows all rose in a wild black scatter from the branches of the tree and flapped and circled like heavy black shadows in the sky. They did not notice that the wild-crow music grew wilder. They did not hear the screaming crows.

But the Bunny No Good did. All this he saw and heard as he dreamed in the immense folding leaves of the cabbage. He knew something was happening. And sure enough . . .

There came sneaking through the cornfield a red fox. The crows saw him, and the Bunny No Good saw the crows. Should he get down out of his cabbage and thump his hind legs on the ground to warn the other eleven hundred little bunnies?

Not yet.
It was still early in the morning.
He made a song to himself about crows:

> *"Crows, crows,*
> *Old black crows*
> *Nobody knows*
> *Where the red fox goes.*
> *Nobody knows*
> *But the wild black crows."*

The crows circled black across the sky, leaving the tree-tops empty.

The red fox came creeping through, one paw lifted and another paw down, sniffing the cold moist air, delicately sniffing the breeze on which he could smell eleven hundred warm little rabbits.

This was no dream.

The Bunny No Good jumped out of his cabbage. He banged his hind legs thump on the ground—*thump*—then he ran like a weasel to the other eleven hundred little bunnies and they all dove headfirst into their holes in the ground where they were safe.

The fox came sniffing along, and he saw nothing but eleven hundred little rabbit tracks and little holes in the ground, so he went away. And pretty soon Bunny Bun Bun poked his head out and saw that the fox was gone and even his scent had blown away across the land after him.

So he told the others, and eleven hundred little bunny heads popped out of their holes, and soon they were all hopping about as usual.

"Someone saved our lives," squeaked the eleven hundred little rabbits.

"Bravo!" called Bunny Bun Bun.

"Caw-caw-caw," screeched the crows.

But the Bunny No Good had gone back to his cabbage. His little red eyes blinked dreamily in his square fur face. And there he sat dreaming away in the immense folding leaves of the cabbage.

It was still very early in the morning.

# Snow White and Rose Red

## by the Brothers Grimm
## retold by Rose Dobbs

 poor widow lived with her two daughters in a cottage at the edge of a forest. In front of the cottage stood two rose trees. Each year one bore beautiful white roses; the other, lovely red roses.

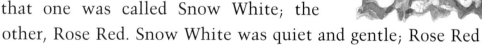

The two girls were so like the roses that one was called Snow White; the other, Rose Red. Snow White was quiet and gentle; Rose Red

 was merry and gay. Snow White liked to stay home helping her mother or reading. Rose Red liked to run about in the fields and meadows, chasing butterflies and picking flowers. Although they were so different, both sisters were good and kind and loved each other dearly.

Often they would go together into the forest to gather berries. They were never afraid, for the wild forest creatures were their friends and never startled or harmed them. Shy rabbits would nibble cabbage leaves out of their hands; pretty fawns grazed peacefully by their side; and at their approach, birds never flew away, but sang merrily on.

Snow White and Rose Red were good little housekeepers. They kept their mother's cottage so neat and clean that it was a pleasure to enter it. In the summertime, Rose Red dusted and swept every morning. Then she picked a nosegay for her mother, always remembering to put into it a white rose and a red rose. During the cold winter, it was Snow White who rose early, lit the fire, and put the kettle on to boil. The kettle was made of brass, but it was so brightly polished that it shone like gold.

When the snow fell in big soft white flakes, mother and daughters liked to sit before the fire. The mother would read out of a big book stories of kings and princes, witches and fairies, while the girls spun busily and listened spellbound. One evening, when they were sitting thus cozily, there came a knock at the door.

"Quick, Rose Red," said the mother. "Open the door. Perhaps it is a traveler, seeking shelter this bitter cold night."

Rose Red unbolted the door, but instead of a weary traveler there stood in the doorway a big black shaggy bear. Rose Red screamed, and Snow White ran and hid behind her mother's bed. Rose Red tried to close the door, but the bear began to speak. "Don't be afraid," he said. "I won't harm any of you. I am cold and tired and only want to warm myself and rest a while."

"Oh, you poor bear," cried the mother. "Come in by all means and warm yourself. But be careful lest a spark from the fire singe your furry coat."

"I'd like the snow brushed off me first," said the bear.

So the mother called Snow White, who came out timidly from behind the bed, and to both children she said, "Take your little brooms and brush the snow off the bear. Don't be afraid. He won't hurt you."

This they did, and then the bear came into the room. He stretched himself before the fire and grunted in contentment. He was friendly and gentle, and before long the girls were quite at home with him. They came closer and growing bolder began to romp with him and to tease him. They even beat him playfully with a hazel twig. Once when they spanked a little too hard, the bear cried out, "Spare my life, dear children:

*Snow White, Rose Red,*
*Do not beat your wooer dead.*"

The children had no idea what this meant so they paid little attention. The bear spent the night, and in the morning he left. He trotted over the snow into the forest, but before night fell he came back. And so throughout the long winter, the bear went out in the morning and returned before dark. The children became so used to him that they left the door unbolted until their shaggy friend had come in.

One morning soon after the snow had melted and spring had turned the world soft and green again, the bear said to Snow White, "When I leave you today it will be for a long time, for I shall be gone all summer."

"Where must you go then, dear bear?" asked Snow White

sadly, for she knew she would miss him.

"I must go into the forest to guard my treasure so that it won't fall into the hands of the wicked dwarfs," the bear told her. "In the winter, when the ground is frozen hard, the dwarfs cannot break through, and so my treasure is safe. But now that the sun's warmth has softened the earth, the dwarfs will come out of their holes to steal everything they can."

Snow White was very sad at the thought of not seeing the bear again. She opened the door slowly, and the bear, hurrying through, caught his fur on the latch and tore a hole in his coat. It seemed to Snow White that a golden gleam shone through the hole, but she could not be sure and she couldn't ask because the bear was already out of sight.

Not long after that, the children went into the forest to gather firewood. As they walked about, they came to a tree lying across the path, and near its trunk something was jumping up and down in the grass. Curious, the children went up to the trunk to see what it might be. When they came near, they saw a little old wrinkled dwarf with a long white beard,

the end of which was caught in a crack in the tree.

The little man hopped up and down and pulled and tugged but could not free himself. He glared at the girls and snapped, "Well, are you just going to stand there and not help me?"

"Poor little man, what have you done?" asked Rose Red.

"Done?" snarled the dwarf. "I haven't done anything, you stupid goose. I needed a bit of wood for my fire to cook my simple little meal and was just about to cut into the tree when my hand slipped, the wedge I had put in flew out, and my beautiful white beard got caught in the crack and I cannot get away."

The children tried very hard, but they could not free the beard. At last Rose Red said, "I'll go and get some help."

"Oh, you idiots!" sputtered the dwarf in a rage. "You white-faced fools! What good will other mortals do me? There are two too many of you now. Think of something better."

"Don't be so impatient," said Snow White. "I have thought of something." And she took her scissors out of her pocket and cut off the end of the beard.

The moment he felt himself free the dwarf snatched up a sack of gold that lay between the roots of the tree. He threw it over his shoulder and marched off, grumbling to himself: "Stupid ninnies! The idea! Cutting off my beautiful beard. Bad luck to them!"

A day or so later, Snow White and Rose Red went out to catch a few fish for supper. As they came to the pond, they saw something that looked like a giant grasshopper hopping about on the bank, dangerously close to the water. They ran up and recognized the dwarf.

"You'll fall into the pond if you aren't careful," said Rose Red.

"I'm not such a fool as that," snapped the dwarf. "Don't you see that the fish at the end of my line is trying to pull me in?"

The dwarf had been fishing at the pond's edge, when a strong wind arose, hopelessly entangling his beard and the fishing line. Just then the dwarf had felt a tug and knew he had caught a fish, but the fish was too big and the little man could not pull him out. Instead it looked as if any moment the fish was going to pull him into the water, unless something happened quickly to help him.

Snow White and Rose Red tried to free the beard from the line, but they couldn't do it. So again Snow White took out her scissors and cut off another piece of the long white beard. Instead of being grateful, the dwarf was furious. "You donkey," he stormed. "Are you trying to have me disowned by my people? How can I face them with most of my beautiful white beard gone? You should have worn your feet out before you ran up to me." Snatching up a sack of pearls which lay in the rushes, he dragged it away, muttering and grumbling.

Some time after this Snow White and Rose Red went to town to buy for their mother needles and thread, laces and ribbons. Their way led through a field where great rocks lay strewn about. Overhead they noticed an eagle flying round and round. Slowly it circled and lower it came until suddenly it swooped down behind an enormous rock. At once the children heard a loud frightened cry and, running up, were horrified to find that the huge bird was carrying off their ill-tempered friend, the dwarf. Snow White seized the little man's coat and Rose Red his beard, and they tugged and pulled so hard that at last the bird gave up the struggle, let go, and flew off.

As soon as he recovered from his fright, the dwarf began

to scold as usual. "You clumsy creatures," he ranted. "Couldn't you have been more careful? Look at my coat. It's in shreds. Fools!" He picked up a bag of precious stones and, grumbling all the while, went off to his hole in the ground.

The girls, quite used to the dwarf's bad manners by this time, continued on their way and made their purchases. On the way home, they had to cross the same field. When they came to the place of the big rock, they were surprised to see the dwarf there. He had emptied the sack of gems in a clean spot on the ground, certain that no one would come by at that time of day. The late afternoon sun shone on the gems, making them glow and sparkle with every color of the rainbow. They were so beautiful that Snow White and Rose Red had to stop and admire them.

"What are you gaping at?" shrieked the little man in a frenzy. Before he could say another word, a deep growl was heard, and out of the forest came a big black shaggy bear. The terrified dwarf tried to make for his cave, but the bear got in his way. Then, very frightened, he whined: "Spare me, dear bear, I am such a skinny little fellow I wouldn't even make an appetizer for you. Spare my life and you shall have my treasure—all this and everything I have hidden in my cave. Take these two wicked girls instead. They're nice and plump and will make a satisfying meal."

The bear paid no attention to the dreadful little man. He gave him one blow with his huge paw, and the dwarf did not move again.

By this time Snow White and Rose Red had started to run away, but the bear called after them. "Snow White! Rose Red! Wait for me. I'll not harm you." They knew that voice—it was their old friend of the forest. The girls waited for him, and as soon as he came up to them a wonderful thing happened. His shaggy black coat fell off, and there before them stood a handsome young prince, clad in shining gold.

"I am a king's son," he told them. "That wicked dwarf had bewitched me and put me under a spell to roam the forest until his death would set me free. Now he has been punished as he richly deserved."

Snow White married him and Rose Red married his brother, and they divided between them the treasure that the dwarf had collected. The old mother went to live with her children. She brought with her the two rose trees, and every year they continued to bloom, one with beautiful white roses, the other with lovely red roses.

# ACKNOWLEDGMENTS

*Grateful acknowledgment is made to the following for permission to reprint previously published material:*

"The Baker's Cat" from *A Necklace of Raindrops* by Joan Aiken. Copyright © 1968 by Joan Aiken. Used by permission of Doubleday, a division of Bantam Doubleday Dell Publishing Group, Inc.

"The Dreaming Bunny" from *The Golden Sleepy Book* by Margaret Wise Brown. Copyright 1971, 1948 by Western Publishing, Inc. Used by permission.

*Follow the Wind* by Alvin Tresselt. Copyright 1950 by Lothrop, Lee & Shepard Co., Inc. Published by Lothrop, Lee & Shepard, Inc. Reprinted by permission of William Morrow and Company, Inc./Publishers, New York.

*Grumley the Grouch* by Marjorie Weinman Sharmat. Text copyright © 1980 by Marjorie Weinman Sharmat. Used by permission of M. B. & M. E. Sharmat Trust.

"The Lad Who Went to the North Wind" from *The Three Sillies and 10 Other Stories to Read Aloud* by Anne Rockwell. Copyright © 1979 by Anne Rockwell. Selection reprinted by permission of HarperCollins Publishers.

*The Man Who Had No Dream*, idea by Kjell Ringi, written by Adelaide Holl. Text copyright © 1969 by Random House, Inc. Reprinted by permission of Random House, Inc.

*Under the Moon* by Joanne Ryder. Text copyright © 1989 by Joanne Ryder. Used by permission of Random House, Inc.

"Snow White and Rose Red" from *Grimm's Fairy Tales*, retold by Rose Dobbs. Text copyright © 1955 by Rose Dobbs. Text copyright renewed 1983 by Rose Dobbs. Reprinted by permission of Random House, Inc.

"Young Kate" from *The Little Bookroom* by Eleanor Farjeon. Copyright © 1955 by Eleanor Farjeon. Published by Puffin Books, Ltd. Reprinted by permission of David Higham Associates, Ltd.

## ABOUT THE ILLUSTRATOR

Jane Dyer is an award-winning illustrator who lives in western Massachusetts with her husband, Tom, and their daughters, Brooke and Cecily. She works in a studio that overlooks gardens and a lily pond designed by her husband. Several of the stories in *The Random House Book of Bedtime Stories* were childhood favorites of hers.